Baking and Entering

Milly's Magical Midlife

Janet Butler Male

Published by Janet Male, 2021.

This is a work of fiction. Similarities to real people, places, or events are entirely coincidental.

BAKING AND ENTERING

First edition. June 15, 2021.

Copyright © 2021 Janet Butler Male.

Written by Janet Butler Male.

Liverpool, 1987

I pulled the official-looking letter from my handbag, gingerly opened the seal and, heart in mouth, scanned the contents.

'Yes! My divorce is final,' I shrieked, unable to contain my excitement.

Everyone on the crowded bus into Liverpool turned and stared at me.

Whoops! 'Sorry,' I mumbled

'Wish I'd divorced years ago,' said the passenger next to me as she removed her transparent rain bonnet. It was a drizzly day in May and the bus smelled of diesel fumes and damp.

'Are you still married?' I asked dutifully.

'Yes – the bugger's still alive.'

I laughed. 'How long have you known him?'

'My whole blooming life, queen. I married Bert in 1931 when I was eighteen. I hate to admit it, but my happiest time was when he was called up.'

Strangers have always confided in me, whether I want them to or not. 'World War Two?' I said.

'Yes. Bert's not a bad old stick, but everything has to be his way.'

'Tell me about it.'

She took me literally and launched into great detail about Bert's 'annoying ways'.

'He has to have an Eccles cake after his tea on Tuesdays. Would the world end if he had a cream cake?'

'Will only wear green socks...'

'Can't put my clothes in with his in the washing machine. Mind you; I ignore that...'

Amused and intrigued, I overshot my stop then ran to work.

The despotic manager of Feet First insisted everyone was 'on the floor' by 8.50 am *sharp*. I missed the deadline by thirty seconds, and the gimlet-eyed woman, stopwatch in hand, screamed in a broad Scouse accent, 'You're late, and I won't have it!'

'Sorry,' I mumbled, not wishing to increase Miss Harridan's wrath. 'You look lovely today. Is that a new outfit?'

Miss Harridan patted her helmet-like shampoo and set and looked down at the tight linen dress which strained over her burgeoning tummy. 'Yes, it's a present from my boyfriend. He likes me in pink.'

'It suits you,' I said.

Flush with flattery, Miss Harridan waddled away.

'You're such a liar,' said Cheryl, a co-worker. 'It looks awful with her red hair and beetroot face.'

'I know, but I needed to flatter her so she wouldn't stop my morning break.'

'Any news of the divorce?'

'Tell you later. Get the duster and polish out; Miss Harridan is on the prowl.'

BAKING AND ENTERING

During morning break, I escaped to the Ringo Cafe. I settled into a corner table with a large mug of tea and an iced bun, hoping for peace to read my Margery Allingham mystery. But Cheryl appeared, plonked herself at my table and said, 'Put that book away and spill the beans.'

'About what?'

'The divorce. I saw the glint in your eye.'

'You'd make a brilliant detective. The postie delivered the decree absolute as I rushed out the door this morning. I opened the letter on the bus and made a fool of myself.'

'How come?'

'I screamed out loud.'

'With joy, I hope?'

'Of course.'

Cheryl's kind eyes met mine. 'Congratulations – you've wanted rid of him for years.'

'You make it sound like I considered murder.'

'Did you?'

'Only in my mind.'

'Isn't that where murders begin?'

'Touché.'

'How do you feel?'

'Young, free and forty,' I said.

'Better than young, free and fifty.'

'Who's fifty?'

'You, if you'd waited another ten years.'

'God forbid. Why did I wait so long?'

'Beats me.'

After the break, as I tidied endless shoes, I thought back. I hadn't wanted to marry Steve but got carried along on a conveyor belt of preparation and excitement – the white satin gown, bridesmaids, bridesmaid dresses, venue, photographer.

Steve was nice enough but didn't light my fire. Not like Mike had. Mike made my spirit soar when he entered the room. Every moment with him fizzed.

But Mike betrayed me – died when a balcony collapsed when he was in Valencia with his mates.

Steve, who I'd met at junior school, was there to dry my tears. So I married him for comfort and reassurance. Spent twenty years with him because he was too pleasant to upset.

When Steve hit forty recently, he announced his daring plan to tour America on a motorbike. Steve! The man who thought it exciting to go above fifty miles per hour in his Ford Fiesta. The man who believed it was daring to have an extra biscuit with a cup of tea. The man who thought a four-bar Kit Kat was risqué. 'It's a bit naughty, Milly. A two-bar would suffice.'

'Break away,' I said of the proposed motorbike tour, deliberately using a biscuit reference that flew over his head.

'Are you sure?'

'Yes.'

'You don't mind riding pillion?'

No way. If I did an American road trip it would be in a red Ford Mustang convertible, a sexy man at my side. My face must have shown horror, as Steve immediately relented. 'Only kidding. I'm going with a few mates. It's been our dream since we saw *Easy Rider* at the Odeon. And I won't dip into our funds – Dad said he'll slip me a few quid in exchange for painting the outside of his and Mum's house. Are you sure you don't mind?'

'Of course not.' I resisted a happy jig in anticipation of precious alone time. 'Shall we go out for dinner to chat about your fab trip, Steve?'

'But it's not either of our birthdays.'

'You're about to tour America on a bike; surely you can be spontaneous about a restaurant,' I teased. 'I'll book The Queen's Table.'

'It's a bit posh there. The Little Chef would be cheaper.'

'We're planning your trip of a lifetime, not having a quick snack before we paint a wall.'

'I suppose.'

Over Steak Diane and red wine, we discussed what we should have twenty years prior – our relationship – or lack of. Turned out, we'd both dreamed of freedom but didn't want to cause upset and had endured a dull existence of almost zero passion and heightened politeness.

John Debrett, of *Debrett's Etiquette and Modern Manners* fame, would be proud.

We also hadn't wanted to upset our daughter, silly as Kaye was independence personified and moved to Northumberland to live with her boyfriend at seventeen.

Over Black Forest Gateau, we decided to get divorced.

Still friends, we opted to live together until the house sold. I bagged the main bedroom, and Steve moved to our daughter's old room.

'It never was a girlie bedroom anyway. Not with our little tomboy,' he said.

Finally, we'd admitted we were more like brother and sister than husband and wife.

Now, the divorce had come through while Steve was on his dream trip.

I wanted to live in London but couldn't afford to. Once we sold the marital abode and divided the proceeds, I'd have enough for a small house or flat in the north of England or a garage or broom cupboard in London.

'Have you got these in size five, love?' said a blonde woman brandishing a black patent court shoe.

'I'll check the stockroom, madam.'

Many feet, shoes, a bus ride and a short walk later, I reached my small semi-detached house in Fairley, a Liverpool suburb. I pushed open my front door with effort due to a thick envelope lodged underneath. Why hadn't the postman given it to me earlier?

'Hello!' shouted Mrs Snoops from over the fence. 'The postie delivered one of your letters to me, and I shoved it through your letterbox. It looked posh. Fancy a cuppa?'

Gosh, she was nosy. 'Perhaps later. My feet are killing me, and I must sit down.'

I intuited the latest letter was important, so in honour of its opening ceremony, I put the kettle on, changed into floral pyjamas and furry slippers, then sat down with a cup of tea and a bourbon biscuit in front of the gas fire. For May, it was Baltic.

'What can this be?' I said to my fluffy brown cat, Colin, as I waved the cream envelope. 'It looks important.'

'Meow!'

'I'm glad you agree.'

Carefully, I opened the seal and pulled out a thick sheet of cream paper. At its top was a raised logo: *Crown and Scimitar Solicitors, The Strand, London.*

Impressive.

As I read further, my heart leapt with sadness, joy, and disbelief. Sadness that an old friend had died, joy and disbelief she had left me a hundred thousand pounds – and a two-bedroom flat in South Kensington.

Hang about. That couldn't be right. A fortune and a flat in a posh part of London?

Someone was having a laugh at my expense.

I pinched myself and re-read the letter.

Did fairy tales come true? Could this be real?

The friend was Priscilla Hodgkin – Prill – who had owned Togs boutique in Liverpool and was my first boss. When we first met, I was sixteen, and Prill was in her fifties. She thought I had great potential and was disappointed when I plumped for Steve. 'He's a fuddy-duddy, darling, and will make you old before your time. You're on the rebound from Mike, so please wait awhile.'

In 1977, Prill sold Togs and moved to a seaside village in Sussex as her beloved husband wished to spend his days pottering in the garden. 'I can't think of anything more dull, darling,' she said when she broke the news.

Prill and I never met again but kept in touch over the phone. Ironically, her husband keeled over and died of an instant heart attack in 1980 while watering a hydrangea bush.

'I always said gardening was bad for him,' Prill said in a voice cracked with grief.

About six months ago, Prill said, 'I've left you a little something in my will, Milly.'

Flattered, I thought she meant a pearl necklace I'd once admired. But a hundred thousand pounds and a London flat – wow!

I was devastated that Prill was dead, and during our last phone call two months earlier, she sounded healthy and vibrant. Strange. And the solicitor's letter didn't mention the cause of death. But why would it?

There was a loud rap at the front door, which I answered as I pasted on a fake smile. 'Come in, Mrs Snoops. Fancy a Babycham?'

'Ooh, lovely. I'd imagined Tetley tea and a custard cream. What are we celebrating?'

'My divorce.' I didn't mention the inheritance, or it would be all around Fairley by morning.

Is it True?

In bed, released from the usual money worries, I fell asleep fast but woke at 3 am. Was the letter a hoax? Surely not, as it seemed genuine. Or maybe not.

The clock hands crawled as my tummy churned. Tomorrow was my day off, so I could call the solicitor without sneaking behind Miss Harridan's back.

But the good news was too good to be true. Convinced I was the victim of a cruel scam, I fell into a fitful sleep and woke at 8 am.

Damn, it was at least an hour before Crown and Scimitar opened, so I made a cup of tea, ran a hot lavender-scented bath and languished as I imagined a decadent life, followed by squalor. My mind tricked me into thinking the news was true, then false, then true.

Dressed for the day in a black A-line skirt and a cream sweater, I dialled a London number as I bit my lip.

'Crown and Scimitar,' said a plummy female voice – very Miss Moneypenny.

'May I speak to Mr Crown? It's Mrs Miller about my surprise inheritance.'

'He's expecting your call – I'll put you through.'

After what seemed an eternity but was probably thirty seconds, a gravelly voice like Mr Kipling's (the man from the cake ads) said, 'Hello, Mrs Miller. Congratulations on your good fortune.'

'It's true?'

'Of course. We don't dispatch fake letters. After a few security checks, we can issue a cheque.'

'Wow.'

'Should we post the deeds and keys to your Fairley address, or would you prefer to collect them from our office?'

'I'll pick them up tomorrow,' I surprised myself. 'May I stay in the flat for a few days?'

'Mrs Miller, stay for the rest of your life if you wish. I visited yesterday, and it's clean, aired, and ready to go as the cleaner, Dolly, still visits. She's the only potential problem.'

'Problem?' Oh, no, I knew it was too good to be true.

'As a condition of the will, you must employ Dolly for at least a year for eight hours a week, five pounds an hour.'

I'd never had a cleaner, and the idea was decadent. But if I didn't like her, I could go out while Dolly cleaned. Not a hardship with lovely London at my feet – shops, museums and its general city wonderfulness. And I could certainly afford the wages.

I hadn't planned to go to London the next day, but as the words fell from my mouth, I knew it was what I wanted. And I had a day to get organised.

First, I phoned work, and Cheryl answered. 'Hello. Feet First. How may I help you?'

'Hi, Cheryl. It's me – Milly. Can you get Miss Harridan on the phone?'

'She's got a cob on. Is it important?'

'Yes. I'm not coming into work until next week.'

'She'll go crazy. You know she needs at least four weeks' notice of time off.'

'Then she'll go crazy. Please fetch her, Cheryl.'

'Okay, but it's your funeral. Hang on a mo.'

Miss Harridan barked, 'Hello, Milly. To what do I owe this *pleasure*?'

'A friend of mine died, and I need a few days off.'

A long silence.

I held my breath.

'Was he or she a relative?'

'Not exactly.'

'The answer is no. I expect the next few days to be extra busy.'

She would, wouldn't she? Her middle name was Awkward. Throat dry, I stood my ground. 'I have days owing.'

'If you take time off, don't return.'

Heart aflutter, I blurted, 'Then I officially hand in my notice with immediate effect.'

I replaced the receiver, did a lap of honour around the living room, then fell onto the gold dralon sofa beside the cat and said, 'We're off to London, Colin.'

Colin glared. Oh, dear. Perhaps London wasn't the best place for an adventurous feline. He liked to go out and was safe in the quiet cul-de-sac. Or so I told myself.

The phone rang. Cheryl. 'What did you say to Miss Harridan? She stormed out in a rage.'

'I handed in my notice.'

A loud gasp. 'Have you got another job?'

'No.'

'Then, why?'

Cheryl was an ally, and I wanted to treat her well. Didn't wish to be a person who got rich then dropped their mates. Although there were a few people I'd be glad to drop, such as my ex-mother-in-law who thought the sun shone from Steve's rear end, and I was the devil incarnate. 'I have to go away for a few days. What are you doing next Tuesday evening?'

'I have a hot date with Bobby Ewing.'

Dallas – the soap everyone loved or loved to hate. 'Bobby can wait. I'll treat you to dinner at Oodles of Noodles. You love their sweet and sour pork.' So did I.

'Thanks, but why?'

'Tell you next week.'

After quick ablutions, I nipped into town on the bus, forever wary of parking in central Liverpool, which was expensive and tricky. I wouldn't need a car in London with its fab public transport system and black cabs. I hated the thought of the tube after dark due to the scary thrillers and mysteries I liked to watch and read.

In the British Home Stores cafe, I enjoyed sausage, egg and chips. In George Henry Lee, my favourite department store, I bought some new clothes, avoiding those with enormous shoulder pads as I was not a fan of the craze. I even went mad and bought a pair of jeans, having never worn them before. Before returning home, I bought a return train ticket to London Euston from Lime Street. First class! Why not?

I was on my way.

London

'Mr Crown will see you now,' said his assistant as she looked down her long nose with narrowed ice-blue eyes.

I got the distinct impression she disliked me, and her pinched expression hinted at jealousy.

Mr Crown looked how he sounded – a kind, elderly gentleman. However, he didn't offer me any Mr Kipling cakes with my coffee, but a choice of rich tea or digestive biscuits.

And he was super organised. In my excitement, I hadn't thought about home insurance, but he'd thought of everything. Soon after signing a few documents, Mr Crown gave me the flat's keys; then a black cab took me to South Kensington – figuring out the tube and buses could wait.

When the taxi stopped at a tall white-painted terrace on the wide, tree-lined Queen Avenue, I thanked the chatty driver, paid the fare along with a tip and faced my new home.

After I climbed six marble steps to a large red front door, I turned a brass key and entered a spacious communal hall with a black-and-white marble chessboard floor. A large crystal vase of fragrant lilacs on a mahogany shelf added to the aura of tasteful decadence.

On stairs carpeted with grey Wilton, I lugged my blue Samsonite suitcase upstairs.

As I reached the first landing, a slim doe-eyed girl, about twenty-six, hurtled downwards like the Road Runner, screeched to a halt and said, 'Can I help with that?'

'No, it's okay.'

'Are you sure?'

'Yes.'

I'm Fawn, and I live in 28b. I just fed the fish on the top floor.'

'Milly Miller.' I wasn't sure whether to comment on the fish or Fawn's familiar lilt and opted for the latter. 'You're from Liverpool?'

'Yes – so are you, judging by your accent.'

'Busted.' In mock surrender, I held up my hands.

'Are you moving into 28c?'

'Yes.'

'Such a shame the nice old lady died there.'

Sick bile rose in my throat. 'In this building?'

'Yes.'

'I thought she died in Piddleton-on-Sea.' I had merely surmised.

'No.'

'What did she die from?'

Fawn clutched her slender throat. 'Did nobody tell you?'

'No.'

'She drowned in the bath – the verdict was accidental death.'

'How awful.' Dizzy, I clutched the mahogany bannister for support.

'Let me help with that.' Fawn picked up my suitcase as if it were filled with feathers and bounded upstairs on her Bambi legs, as I struggled to keep pace. Outside 28c, I pulled another brass key from my handbag and popped it in the lock. As I opened the door, the fragrance of beeswax furniture polish welcomed me.

A small hall led to a large living room with a high ceiling, crown mouldings and a crystal chandelier. Two tall windows had heavy coral and blue floral drapes finished with swags and tails. The carpet was blue wool with a deep underlay, and the entire space was pure elegance.

'It's like something from one of those posh interior magazines,' I said.

'Funny you should say that. *Yuppie Style* featured it last year.'

An enormous vase of fragrant red roses and gypsophila sat on an oak coffee table, and a log fire burned in the ornate grate. 'Oh, a real log fire,' I exclaimed.

'No, it's gas, but a brilliant imitation.'

Enraptured and overcome, I fell onto one of two blue velvet chesterfield sofas.

'Dolly probably just left and forgot to turn off the fire,' said Fawn.

'Dolly?'

'Yes, the cleaner.'

'Oh, of course.'

'She's a hoot. Must go as I'm late for work.'

'Where do you work?'

'I manage Blossoms Cafe on King's Road, Chelsea. Pop in for dinner later. I'm allowed to give friends and family twenty per cent off.'

'Thanks – but I'm only good for brandy, bath and bed.' I'd spotted a bottle of Courvoisier in the drinks cabinet, a treat usually reserved for Christmas.

'Come to Blossoms for coffee and croissants tomorrow morning.'

Always the polite hostess, I said, 'Would you like to come here instead?'

'I'd love to, but a waitress is off sick with gastric flu, and I'm on double shifts. Can I get your brandy before I go?'

'It's okay, thanks – I'll manage.'

She hesitated, then said, 'Don't be scared the old lady died here.'

'I'm not,' I lied.

'Good. See you soon.' Fawn rushed away and moments later I heard the front door slam shut. The girl was a whirlwind.

After I finished a balloon of delicious brandy, I fancied a bath. But someone had died in it. Don't be silly, I told myself, the body wouldn't be in the tub, and I couldn't avoid the room forever. Maybe I should sell the property.

But that couldn't happen immediately.

Nervously, I rose from the sofa and ventured along the narrow rose-painted hallway. The first door opened to a small but stylish kitchen/diner, the second to a spacious yellow and blue bedroom. Mine.

I returned to the living room, rescued my suitcase and plonked it on the large bed. Quickly, I undressed and unearthed my well-worn blue candlewick dressing gown which travelled everywhere with me. Not that I'd travelled much, hadn't even set foot out of England. Steve had always been reluctant to travel abroad. 'What if I get a gippy tummy?' Another reason I was shocked when he went to America.

After gathering courage, I entered the corridor again. The next door hid a large airing cupboard, and I took a plush and warm cream bath sheet off a neat shelf. I opened the next door – and screamed, ran to the living room, grabbed my keys, then fled downstairs barefoot where I battered at the ground-floor flat's door.

Let someone be home, I prayed.

A cherubic man, mid twenties, with the body of Adonis and a halo of blonde curls appeared. It was as if he'd stepped straight from *Vogue* or a Rossetti painting. 'What on earth is the matter?' he said.

'There's a dead woman in my bathtub.'

'And you are?'

'Milly Miller – the new resident of 28c.'

'Sebastian. I thought the scream was next door's telly as the owner is deaf and has it loud. Let's investigate.'

Somewhat shocked, I mumbled, 'Thanks.'

I couldn't believe he was called Sebastian. If you've seen Anthony Andrews as Lord Sebastian Flyte in *Brideshead Revisited,* you'll know who *this* Sebastian looked like – the only thing missing was Aloysius – the teddy bear.

The cherub climbed the stairs ahead of me as I admired his perfect posterior clad in tight light-blue jeans.

A woman is dead, while you ogle a young man's bum, I scolded myself. But you'd have to be dead not to admire that perfect backside.

Heart in mouth, I cowered in the living room until Sebastian went to investigate.

Soon he reappeared with a grin. 'You daft thing – Dolly was asleep in the bath.'

'Why didn't she hear my screams?'

'She had headphones on.'

Mortified, I said, 'Fawn said the previous owner died in the bath, and when I saw...'

'Shall we sit here and wait for Dolly to emerge from the deep?'

'Yes, but it's embarrassing.'

'Why?'

'We both saw her naked.'

'People are normally naked in baths.' He winked as I felt myself blush. Oh, the thought of this Adonis naked was too much for my ageing hormones. 'You know what I mean,' I blustered.

'Once you've met Dolly, you'll know there is no need for embarrassment.'

'Why?'

'You'll see.' His divine blue eyes twinkled.

It was easy to chat with Sebastian as he did most of the talking. Within minutes, I knew he was a trust-fund kid and lived with his 'sexy' boyfriend, a plumber. 'I met him when he came to fix a dripping tap last month, and he never left. I'll introduce you when he gets home from work. But I have a photo in my wallet.'

He pulled a brown calf leather wallet from his shirt pocket and opened it to show a dark-haired man of about thirty.

'He's good looking,' I said dutifully, but he was a moth compared to Sebastian, the butterfly.

'Hello, duckies!' said a confident female voice.

A fiftyish woman wearing a feather-trimmed pink cardigan, pink trousers, giant chandelier earrings and crimson lipstick sashayed into the room. She had blonde bouffant hair and reeked of hairspray and a cloying, sweet floral fragrance.

'You must be Dolly.' I rose to shake her hand.

'Sit down, ducks. You must have been traumatised to see me in my birthday suit. My skin needs a good iron.'

'There were too many bubbles to see much,' I admitted truthfully.

'I tipped half a bottle of rose bubble bath under the tap.'

'Do you usually bathe while on duty?' I emulated a convent's mother superior but didn't want to be walked over from the outset and set a precedent. After all, I'd inherited Dolly.

'Wouldn't dream of it, ducks, but the boiler blew at home, and the plumber can't come until tomorrow.'

'Perhaps my boyfriend can help,' ventured Sebastian.

'Oh, no, ducks, it's all sorted,' Dolly said hastily. 'Anyone fancy a cuppa?'

'Me,' said a voice from the doorway. 'Is this a private party, or can anyone join in? The door was ajar.'

'Hello, Peter,' chorused Dolly and Sebastian.

A tall, broad man, mid-thirties with a pleasant face stood at the room's entrance.

'Come in. I'm the new resident of this flat.' Gosh, so formal again. What was wrong with me?

'I live on the top floor with my tropical fish. Less trouble than my ex-girlfriend, and I don't have to take them out to dinner.'

'Fawn just fed them,' I said.

'Minx, I asked her to do it earlier while I was at rehearsal. I just arrived home and heard voices on my way upstairs.'

'Are you an actor?'

'No, an opera singer. Fancy a rendition?'

Sebastian winced. 'Not now – you sound like a scalded cat.'

I expected Peter to take offence, but he laughed. 'Don't insult my high C; it's on par with Pavarotti's.'

I liked it here; everyone had a great sense of fun. It felt like coming home, and I wanted to cry with happiness.

When the guests left, I unpacked and, with a happy sigh, fell onto the luxurious mattress. Strangely, I felt more at home here than in the marital abode. As if there was a comforting presence, a kindred spirit. Perhaps it was the ghost of my old friend. *No, don't be silly.*

Tiredness overcame me as I languished. My ex-husband was a martyr to his back, so we'd had a torturous orthopaedic mattress akin to sleeping on bricks. Not that I had ever slept on bricks but they would be cosier than the marital mattress.

I wondered how Steve was fairing on a bike with his bad back and realised I quite missed him. Perhaps absence really did make the heart grow fonder. I should phone him, catch up on the news. Maybe he didn't even know the divorce was final. Gosh – perhaps he had phoned me at home. Guiltily, I picked up the bedside phone and called Mrs Snoops, who was looking after Colin. After two rings, the neighbour said in her poshest voice, 'Hello. The Snoops residence, the lady of the house speaking.'

'Hello, it's Milly. Is Colin okay?'

Normal-voice, she said, 'Of course, you only left this morning. But when I fed him earlier, your answerphone was beeping.'

'Would you pop over and listen to the messages?'

'Already did. I'll get the notes.'

Sometimes nosy neighbours are a boon. I untangled the curled green phone wire as I waited.

Moments later, Mrs Snoops said, 'Your husband and daughter phoned.'

My throat dried. Kaye rarely phoned, too engrossed with her muscled Geordie boyfriend. And why had Steve called?

'I know Kaye's number, but where did my husband call from?'

'Hang on; I wrote that down on a soup packet – Campbell's Cocakleekie.'

Steve was in the John Wayne Motel on Route 66, and he and I had the best chat we'd had in years. Perhaps ever. How strange. That he was doing something exciting made him seem more interesting. And I hadn't planned to mention my windfall until he said, 'I'm coming home early as I've run out of money. It's a pity our house hasn't sold yet. Any bites?'

'One young couple, but they're in a chain. Can't you work in a bar or something, make a bit of cash?'

'I could, but I'd have to stay behind, as my mates aren't short of dosh. It will be easier to come home than pull pints, knowing they are off to San Francisco on their rented Harleys. I so wanted to do that fantastic CA-1 coast road.'

Without stopping to think, I said, 'I'll wire you five-hundred pounds tomorrow.' There was just over that amount in my savings account until the windfall boosted its balance.

'Have you won the football pools or something?'

'No, ERNIE came up.'

'Have you got a new man already?'

Hardly. 'You know ERNIE stands for Electronic Random Number Indicator Equipment connected with that government premium bond fund.'

'Silly me. How much did you win?'

'Two thousand pounds.' A hunch told me not to say the entire truth yet. 'By the way, I'm in London at a friend's flat.' No need to mention the friend was dead, and the flat mine. All in good time.

'Who's minding Colin?' said Steve.

'Mrs Snoops.'

'The nosy neighbour.'

'We have nothing to hide as our life has been so boring.'

'You're right. I'm sorry, Milly. It's all my fault.'

'It takes two to tango.' *Or not to tango.*

'When I come home, I'll take you dancing.'

'A bit late for that. Our divorce came through.'

A long pause and a slight choking sound.

'Are you alright?' I said, surprised and a little guilty as my main emotion about the divorce was relief.

'Yes, but it's sad as I still love you.'

I didn't see that coming. 'Why didn't you say?'

'The more I didn't say it, the more my throat closed.'

'Well, at least you've said it now. That's nice.' I couldn't return the compliment as I wasn't sure what I felt, apart from sadness over the lacklustre years.

As I was falling asleep, the doorbell rang. Damn. I glanced at the radio alarm, which said 11.59 in huge angry red figures.

Who could it be? I pulled on my old faithful dressing gown and stumbled from my flat (my flat!) and down the stairs. It was okay on the grey Wilton, but as I stepped on marble, my feet froze. Opening the front door, I said, 'Hello, Fawn. Lost your key?'

'Forgot it in my rush. Why did you come downstairs?'

What a silly question. 'To answer the door.'

'Why not use the entryphone?'

'What's an entryphone?'

Fawn rolled her eyes. 'I'll show you in case someone else buzzes in the night.'

In my flat, Fawn demonstrated. 'When it buzzes, pick up the receiver, and if you trust the speaker, press this button, and the front door opens.'

Feeling like a country bumpkin, I said, 'Does it just open the front door?'

'Yes.'

'How will you get into your flat?'

'That key is on a separate keyring I always keep in my handbag.'

'Oh, I see.' I didn't but thought, 'We all have our foibles.'

'Do come to Blossoms for coffee and croissants tomorrow morning – my treat for waking you up. You can't miss it – about five doors along from Peter Jones on King's Road, and it has a large blue awning. Come at about eleven when there's a slight lull before lunch.'

Back in the bedroom, I set the radio alarm for 9 am to give myself time to titivate, then walk to the cafe with the help of my shiny, new *London A-Z* street map.

Blossoms Cafe

Clad in my new togs from George Henry Lee – Gloria Vanderbilt jeans, a cream cotton blouse and a blue gold-buttoned blazer, I popped on a pair of comfy navy loafers from Feet First then stepped into the warmish May sunshine.

After a few wrong turns, I pushed open the door of Blossoms Cafe to a buzz of cheerful chatter and the divine fragrances of cooked breakfasts, fresh-baked pastries, and coffee.

Fawn appeared and gestured to an empty window table. 'Milly! I'm glad you came. Let's sit there, and if I have to work, you can watch the world go by.'

I patted my handbag. 'I always carry a book, so I'm easily entertained.'

We sat at either side of a round table covered in a crisply laundered pink cloth. Fawn summoned a handsome young waiter. 'Peregrine, be a darling and fetch me a cappuccino and two croissants with plenty of butter and jam. What would you like, Milly?'

With a smile at the dazzling young man, I said, 'The same but with marmalade, please.'

Peregrine saluted, clicked his heels and marched away.

'He's a young scamp, hates being told what to do,' said Fawn.

Hiding a smile at Fawn's comparative youth, I said, 'Then, why be a waiter?'

'He's saving for a year in Italy with his girlfriend.'

'The wages must be good.'

'Not really – his family has a second, or is it third, home in Tuscany. He only needs airfare and spending money.'

'How the other half lives.' I forgot I was now nearer the 'other half' than ever before.

I took a sip of cappuccino as my taste buds danced the cancan. 'Oh, my good God, this is the best cappuccino I've ever had.'

'It's the fabulous beans and the extra shot I insist upon,' said Fawn. 'Only about ten per cent of the customers think it too strong and ask for a weaker brew.'

'It's amazing. I almost want to savour it without the croissants.'

'Ah, here they are now. I'm starving,' said Fawn.

With an air of martyrdom, Peregrine delivered two side plates, a basket of flaky pastries, a mountain of butter and oodles of jam and marmalade. Bliss.

Fawn devoured her first croissant, wiped her mouth with a pink paper napkin, then said, 'Priscilla Hodgkin, known as Prill, was murdered in your bathtub.'

Choking on a morsel of delicious buttery pastry, I spluttered, 'How do you know?'

An avalanche of customers fell through the door as Fawn groaned. 'Damn, I'll have to muck in. But I finish at about four today. Can I come to your flat, tell you what I suspect?'

'Of course. I'll have tea and scones at the ready.' In my mind's eye, I saw the calories clocking up, but what the heck. It's not every day you become an heiress.

Mind racing, I scarfed my second delicious croissant then tried to focus on my book – *Death at the Opera*. But I closed it after two pages as I needed my mind off murder, not on it.

I watched the fashionable world go by, *gosh was that Christy Turlington, the supermodel?* Then I waved goodbye to Fawn and walked up Sloane Street towards Harrods. Perhaps a stroll around that famous store would take my mind off gruesome things. Murders were okay in a book or film, but, for real, hideous.

Sloane Street was longer than it looked in the *A-Z,* and I was tired when I reached Harrods. After studying a store plan, I decided to visit the pet department, which had an incredible history. I thought back to articles in various newspapers.

In 1951, Beatrice Lillie, an actress, bought Noel Coward an alligator as a Christmas gift. Imagine unwrapping that. You'd have to make it snappy lest it bit off a finger – or worse.

In 1970, Australian expats John Rendall and Anthony Bourke bought a lion cub they christened 'Christian'. Not surprisingly, he soon outgrew their Chelsea flat, and they released the majestic animal into Kenya's Kora National Park. A year later, they visited Christian, who was ecstatic to see his friends.

After the Endangered Species Act in 1976, Harrods' Pet Kingdom, which opened in 1917, could only offer a less exotic pet collection such as dogs, cats and hamsters. I imagined a mass purr of outrage as Siamese cats heard themselves described as *less exotic.*

Out of the blue, I decided *I* wanted a Siamese cat, and it could live indoors. Colin would never settle in London, and it wouldn't be fair as he loved to go outside and was in and out of the cat flap like a clock's cuckoo. He couldn't access the London flat alone – even via the entryphone. Furthermore, I didn't want him near (or on) the busy London roads, and he was comparatively safe in his Fairley cul-de-sac.

My daughter's phone call had been another request for Colin. 'He's mine, Mum. And we're moving to a farm, so he'll be in feline heaven.'

Perhaps it was time to let Colin go, much as I loved him. Besides, I could always visit now I wasn't laced to Feet First.

As I deciphered the pet department's location, tricky without a compass, the divine aromas of the Food Hall beckoned, and I spent ages in a culinary-delights haze.

Whoops – glancing at the clock above the heavenly bakery counter, I realised it was time to head home – to the London flat, not Fairley.

En route, I nipped into Newsflash and bought *Which Cat?* magazine as I hadn't made it to Harrods' pet department and also imagined their prices would be astronomical. Years of necessary thriftiness had left an indelible mark on my psyche. After Newsflash, I nipped into the Great Escake and bought a large and irresistible custard slice I spotted in the window.

'It's not a custard slice; it's a mille-feuille,' the assistant said to my amusement. Snobbishness usually makes me laugh, never offends me. I nearly bought scones for Fawn's visit, but a hunch said to make them.

At this rate, I'd go up a dress size or three. But diets could wait – I was having fun.

I knew it didn't make sense to add an extra cat to my life as I still had to officially leave Liverpool and decide on Colin's future. But my logic often flies out the window when it comes to pets.

Back home, on a sumptuous sofa with the magazine, a cup of tea and the *custard slice,* I heaved a sigh of absolute bliss.

An hour later, I had narrowed the cat search to two, one in Belgravia, the other in Balham. Not surprisingly, the latter was cheaper. With my windfall, it made little difference but once a bargain hunter, always a bargain hunter.

I phoned the Balham number first, to find the last kitten claimed five minutes earlier. That left the Belgravia option. With trembling fingers, I dialled the number, and a haughty voice said, 'The Farleigh residence, the butler speaking. How may I help you?'

'Are the kittens still for sale?'

'Yes, madam. We have two left.'

'Oh, good. When can I come over?'

'Monday.'

I arranged to arrive on Monday at 11 am, and with delighted anticipation, put the phone down.

Usually, I was more careful with decisions, took my time, but since the windfall I'd been impulsive. Perhaps money was affecting me. Yes, that was it. I wanted to get on with life after living on low rev for years.

I checked my old red-strap Timex watch – 3 pm. Enough time to freshen up and make scones for Fawn's visit. But what was I thinking? I hadn't even bought ingredients. When I checked the cupboards and fridge, I was relieved to find a full plethora of ingredients and kitchenware. Dolly the daily was obviously a treasure.

As I sieved flour, I caught a whiff of lily-of-the-valley mixed with something classy, then a familiar voice said, 'What are you making?'

No. It couldn't be. An ominous chill snaked up my spine as I could swear the voice sounded like my old friend's, the deceased owner of this flat – Priscilla Hodgkin – Prill.

I turned and saw it was indeed Prill – older, slightly transparent, but elegant and fragrant as ever. The room spun as I fell to the floor.

A distant voice said, 'I didn't mean to frighten you, Milly.'

Then I was on a fairground hobby horse as it twirled around and around. The horse turned into a large Siamese cat. But I wasn't at the fair. Where was I?

Stars swam around my brain. Was I at home in Fairley? No, I was in London in the posh flat I'd inherited from an old friend.

I remembered Prill and opened my eyes to find her ghostly version staring at me with concern, and I screamed.

'It's only me, and you know I'd never harm you,' Prill soothed.

Suddenly, I realised there was no need to be scared. Dead or alive, Prill was my good and loyal friend. We all have at least one.

'How long was I out, Prill?'

'About two minutes. You were about to make scones.'

'How do you know?'

'The ingredients and the scone cutter. Do me a favour?'

'Yes?'

'Add a particular ingredient as I miss its fragrance.'

'You have a sense of smell?'

'Yes, strangely enough. Who are the scones for?'

'Fawn from downstairs.'

'Sweet girl, with a touch of the fey. She's an old soul with strong intuition.' Prill pointed. 'You'll find three bottles of Madagascan vanilla at the back of that cupboard behind the Gentleman's relish.'

I ferreted amongst various condiments. 'There's only one.'

'Are you sure?'

After a thorough check, I said, 'Yes.'

Prill frowned. 'How odd. There should be two more.'

'Is it okay to use this one? It's sealed.'

'Yes, go ahead and open it.'

As I unscrewed the top of the tiny bottle and sniffed, elation shot through me, and the final soupcon of fear fled. 'Gosh, this is no ordinary vanilla.'

'No – it has magical qualities,' said Prill.

'What sort of magical qualities?'

'I'll tell you soon.'

When Fawn arrived, she sniffed and said, 'Yum. What's that divine smell?'

'Cherry scones fresh from the oven. Want one?'

'Yes please, although I shouldn't indulge after those croissants then a huge bowl of fettuccine carbonara for lunch. It's the chef's speciality, and I can't resist the creamy, cheesy sauce. May I have a mug of builders' tea?'

'Of course.'

I pulled two green Hornsea Pottery mugs from a kitchen cupboard, but Prill tutted. 'Not mugs, darling. Use the Royal Doulton tea service.'

I gritted my teeth. After years of Miss Harridan's instructions, would it begin again – with a ghost?

What was the point of freedom if I was still bossed about?

Steve wasn't often bossy, nor was I. We had spent our entire marriage stepping around each other. We did what we thought the other wanted – a waste of two lives. Stifled by politeness.

From now, I would do what felt right to me as long as it did not harm good souls. I remembered a phrase from one of my numerous self-help books. *When we are ourselves, we permit others to be their true selves. It's a win-win situation.*

After a deep breath, I said, 'I prefer mugs.'

A triumphant smile lit Prill's face. 'That's the reaction I wanted. Your first step toward never being a mousy doormat again.'

Immediately, I felt taller than my usual five-foot-four.

Although I enjoyed Fawn's jaunty company, I couldn't wait for her to leave so I could chat with Prill who had disappeared to God knows where. The master bedroom? The ether?

I could barely hide my impatience, despite Fawn's lively chatter about numerous boyfriends. How did she remember who was who?

When Fawn said, 'I've got a weekend off soon. James wants me to meet his parents, but Tarquin invited me to a Scottish castle. What should I do?'

'Who do you fancy the most?' I said, sounding fifteen.

'Malcolm, but he's poor.'

'Poor?'

'Relatively speaking, yes. He works offshore as a diver and doesn't have a trust fund. I want to enjoy the high life before I settle down to a life of drudgery.'

'There are other levels between high-life and drudgery. Besides, I thought you were wealthy.'

'No.'

'Then how do you afford this place?' Gosh – I was as nosy as Mrs Snoops.

'It belongs to a boyfriend and I only pay a tiny rent. But I don't know how I'll go back to normal after this. My wages would only pay for a flatshare in a scratty area of London.'

'Perhaps one of your rich men will propose?'

'I doubt it. They have Sloane Rangers like Lady Diana Spencer lined up as future wives.'

'You never know,' I said. 'Anyway, what's this about Prill being murdered?'

Fawn pushed back a lock of dark-blonde hair from her forehead. 'A hunch coupled with logic.'

'Tell me.'

Prill floated into the room and sat on the opposite sofa.

'Can you see her?' I said.

'Of course I can see Fawn,' said Prill.

'See who?' said Fawn.

That answered my question. 'Nobody. Just being daft. Why do you think Prill was murdered?'

Prill leaned forwards.

'I was at my friend's house in Brighton for a few days. Whilst there, I dreamed someone choked Prill while she was in the bath. When I got home, there were police everywhere. The post mortem said she accidentally drowned.'

BAKING AND ENTERING

'And hadn't she?'

'No! The evil murderer made it look that way.'

'How?'

'I don't know yet.' Fawn glanced at her watch. 'Must get ready. James is picking me up at nine, and I need some sleep.'

'Where is he taking you?'

'Dinner then Tramp.'

'Tramp?'

'It's a nightclub.'

'Oh, to be young again,' I lamented when Fawn left.

'Oh, to be alive again,' said Prill.

I giggled. 'Touché.'

Prill, now clad in a cerulean-blue evening gown, crossed her elegant legs and said, 'You're only forty and freshly divorced. It's time you had some fun.'

'With men?'

'One doesn't need men to have fun.'

'Women then?'

'Don't be obtuse. We can have fun alone, as long as we are happy from within. I even intend to have fun as a ghost while I am in this realm. But first, I must solve my murder.'

The hair at the nape of my neck stood to attention. 'You think someone murdered you?'

'I was ninety per cent sure, but Fawn confirmed it.'

'What do you remember about your, erm, death?' I said.

Prill went into a sort of trance, half disappeared, then faded to nothing.

I knew she would return.
At least, I hoped she would.

Prill

It was a Wednesday, and I'd just returned from my solicitor, where I signed a new will favouring Milly. A last-minute decision as I'd planned to leave her a set of pearls she once admired. Everything else was to go to my son, Robbie, but he'd looked possessed the last time I saw him. And he was – by Stella, his evil second wife.

Sadly, Robbie's sweet first wife, Holly, died in a car crash a month before Robbie's second marriage late last year.

The week before Holly died, she invited me to tea in the Glitz Hotel, and I was delighted to accept. Holly was a joy with her sweet heart-shaped face and delightful sense of humour. But at tea, she looked like a vampire had drained her blood.

Over a Limoges teacup, she said, 'This will sound insane. But Robbie is possessed by some awful woman. Until a month ago, he only had eyes for me; now, I barely get a glance. I was convinced he had another woman, but couldn't face the truth.'

'Go on,' I encouraged.

'Last week, I visited a friend, supposedly overnight, but left early because her office summoned her away. I planned to sneak into our house and bed, smother Robbie with kisses. Make him fall in love with me all over again. But as I reached the landing, I heard voices and listened outside the bedroom door. To horrid, vile pillow talk which sucked all the innocence from my soul and filled me with hate.'

My heart nearly stopped. 'Go on.'

Hollow-eyed, Holly said, 'The awful woman said she would murder me, make it look like an accident. Then she and Robbie would marry, murder you, make it look like another accident. Said she had connections and clever methods. Robbie would inherit your estate, and they could both live happily ever after because his financial problems would be over. I was so upset and terrified, I left the house and spent the rest of the night in a hotel. The next day, I told the police, but they thought I was insane, and suggested I saw a doctor.'

'Did you tell Robbie what you heard?' I said.

'No. You're the first person I've told apart from the police. I'm still living with Robbie because I love him, but I must be stupid.'

After reassuring her she was far from stupid and simply in love, I asked Holly about Robbie's financial problems, but she said she didn't know and thought everything was okay.

To my shame, I thought Holly was having a nervous breakdown. But soon after our meeting at the Glitz Hotel, she was dead after the brakes of her beloved Yellow Peril (a TR7) failed.

No way would I let a murdering opportunist inherit a fortune via my son.

For ages, every night before sleep, I saw Holly's frightened face and heard her screams as her out-of-control car hurtled towards the tree.

An indecently short time after Holly's death, my son remarried in Las Vegas and didn't invite me. Further evidence that Holly's story was true. When he got home, he invited me to an expensive lunch, flattered me over Dover sole, but the light had gone from his eyes. I knew he was acting and saw me as a future meal ticket. What had happened? Robbie used to be a nice man, albeit a tad wild. He must have got in with a bad lot. Did he owe money? Had he been gambling again?

I thought I had time to unravel the mystery. It was difficult to see Robbie without Stella, his new wife, as she stuck to him like glue. He clammed up around her as if terrified of saying the wrong thing. When I told a joke, he looked at Stella for permission to laugh. On the few occasions I saw him alone, he said he was happy with his wife. But his frightened eyes told a different story.

After a while, I was no closer to understanding, so I temporarily changed my will and planned to employ a private detective. But I did not plan on dying so soon.

Home from Crown and Scimitar last month, I ran a rose-scented bubble bath, stepped into its soothing depths, closed my eyes and searched for clues about Robbie's changed behaviour. I knew Stella was the key, but I couldn't find the lock. Yes, I would phone a private detective the next day. A close friend had recommended a chap called Barry Brillo, an ex-police detective. 'He's rather scruffy, like Columbo, but equally sharp.'

The bubble bath is the last thing I remember about being alive.

I'd planned to unearth the mystery, get my son from under that woman's clutches, then alter the will in his favour again.

But here I was – a ghost. A ghost determined to get justice and right some terrible wrongs.

How could I explain to Milly? Her life may have been dull before, but at least it was safe. What had I got her into?

And I had to save my son from his evil wife.

I felt terrible for Milly, but at least it was unlikely someone could steal her fortune without marrying her. And she was already married.

Then I remembered. Oh, dear, Milly was divorced.

What had I done?

Please don't say Milly's life is in danger.

Milly. I must get back to her...

Sherlock Holmes

When Prill reappeared, I said, 'Hello.'

'Whoops. I was miles away.'

'You were about to tell me about your death and then disappeared.'

'Disappeared?'

'Faded into the ether. And you're in a different outfit.'

Prill looked down at her coral-pink silk pyjamas and matching marabou-trimmed velvet slippers.

'Aren't you supposed to be naked?' I teased.

'Why naked?'

'In spooky novels and films, the ghosts wear what they died in, and you were in your birthday suit.'

Prill grimaced. 'That would be unseemly.'

'How do you change clothes? Have you a phantom wardrobe?'

'I imagine what I want to wear, and the clothes appear.'

On the coffee table was the latest copy of *Vogue*. Flipping through its pages, I stopped at an alluring advert. 'Can you imagine yourself in this?'

Prill eyed the glossy page.

Moments later, she was in a snazzy black Zandra Rhodes cocktail dress and elegant high-heel shoes.

'Gosh, you even imagined the tights.' I admired the fine-denier hose.

'I would never imagine myself in tights, darling. Only stockings and always silk.'

'You always looked wonderful.'

'I hope I still do. Now, enough about fashion, we have important issues to discuss. You might need a drink.'

After I fetched a glass of white wine and a bowl of peanuts from the kitchen, Prill was back in her silk pyjamas as she languished on a sofa.

I sat opposite and said, 'Spill.'

By the time Prill finished the scary tale, I had refilled my wine glass twice. The copious alcohol helped numb the emotional roller coaster.

'So, you didn't mean to leave me this flat and the money?'

Prill, always direct, said, 'No. As I said, I wanted to solve the mystery, open Robbie's eyes to his wife's evil then change the will. Of course, I'd have still left you the pearls.'

'Do you definitely think Stella was responsible for Holly's death?'

'I would bet my life on it if I were alive.'

Despite the gruesome situation, I grinned as Prill said, 'I'm sorry I got you into this.'

'Don't apologise for leaving me a fortune and this flat.'

'But you might be in danger.'

'No sign of it yet.'

'It's early days.'

'I presume Robbie knows I'm your main heir?'

'No.'

'How come?'

'Something complicated and I suspect not entirely legal I arranged with Mr Crown. Robbie won't hear my will for another few weeks. Mr Crown is a clever man.'

'What did you leave Robbie?'

'Nothing.'

'Really?'

'He will receive a stern letter from Mummy about that awful woman.'

'Won't Robbie visit this flat in a rage when he discovers I inherited it?'

'No. I only bought this place after he married Stella. Robbie thought I still lived in Piddleton-on-Sea. Whenever I met him in London, I pretended I was renting this flat at a peppercorn rent from a sympathetic friend, and Mr Crown will continue that charade.'

'Did Robbie ever visit here?'

'No – we met in restaurants, and I downplayed the decadence of this place – said it was plain but serviceable. I didn't even tell him the address.'

'What will he think happened to the Piddleton-on-Sea house?'

'Mr Crown will say I sold it to pay off debts, and I hope Stella leaves Robbie when she discovers her dastardly plan failed to be lucrative. So perhaps my death was fortuitous.'

Prill didn't mention the Piddleton-on-Sea house again, and I didn't wish to pry.

Lost for words and in need of normality, I scanned the *Radio Times*. 'Fancy a film, Prill? *The Private Life of Sherlock Holmes* starts in five minutes on BBC2.'

'Why not? We might pick up some tips.'

The film was enjoyable, and as the credits rolled, I yawned and Prill said, 'Away to your bed.'

'What about you? Shall I use the spare room?'

The small, cute spare bedroom was at the front of the flat, accessed via a cupboard-like door. 'Don't be silly. Ghosts don't need sleep. I'll spend the night on my honeymoon in Cannes. Bill and I had a divine time, and I have a divine imagination.'

Strangely, I had never met Bill or even seen his photo so I couldn't imagine him. 'Will you imagine the days or the nights?' I said.

'Don't be cheeky. That's private – and X-rated.'

Banters Brasserie

As I lay in bed, I wished I was as clever as Sherlock Holmes – perhaps a pipe would help. There seemed to be endless permutations to this bizarre situation. If Stella had murdered Prill (or paid someone to do it), she would be livid when discovering Robbie had inherited nothing. Zilch. Would she let it go, or would she investigate? And were Mr Crown's machinations against the law?

Had Prill even been murdered? If so, by whom? Could it be someone in this building? Either of their own volition or paid by Robbie and/or Stella?

Brain cogs turning torturously, I fell asleep and woke to the sweet fragrance of Giorgio Beverly Hills. Prill – dressed in a tailored cream suit with a black silk shirt was at the foot of my bed.

'Good morning,' I said. 'You can obviously imagine yourself in any fragrance or outfit.'

'Yes. Who knew being dead was such fun? Come on, rise and shine. I wish to have breakfast in Banters Brasserie.'

I didn't want to be insensitive but had to say, 'Can you eat?'

'No. But I love the aroma and atmosphere in that place. Besides, my son frequents it most Saturday mornings. Hopefully, he will be with Stella, and I'll point them out.'

'We won't be able to chat, or scary men in white coats will drag me to the loonie bin.'

'I've thought of that. In the desk drawer, you'll find a Dictaphone. Pretend to talk into that. Come on, chop-chop. Get dressed.'

I showered, pulled on black trousers and a beige cotton sweater, and we walked to the brasserie. Actually, I walked and Prill sort of floated.

As we entered the restaurant, I fell in lust. My mouth dried, my pulse sped. Who was the divine hunk at the window table? He had come-to-bed hooded grey eyes, curly black hair tinged with silver, and sculpted features. He reminded me of someone, but I couldn't think of who. Perhaps an actor.

Through his fine-knit grey sweater, I noticed pecs of steel. Oh, be still my beating heart. Was he alone? No. As a middle-aged maître d' in an immaculate penguin suit approached to greet me (and Prill), a skinny woman with a sharp pointy face appeared from the ladies' loo and headed to the hunk's table. I christened her Cruella.

The hunk's eyes dimmed as Cruella sat next to him and snapped, 'I hope you managed to order?'

'Not yet.'

'God, you're useless,' she snapped again as his face paled.

'What a cow,' I mulled.

The maître d' addressed me. 'Table for one, madam?'

'As long as it has two chairs because a friend may join me.'

'Right you are. Follow me.'

He led me (and Prill) to a small round table at the edge of the buzzy restaurant, handed me a parchment menu tied with blue ribbon and said, 'I recommend the poached eggs on Brittany-buttered farmhouse toast. I'll send someone to take your order soon.'

As I opened the menu, I said to Prill as she half sat, half hovered in the opposite gilt chair, 'This place is amazing – the buzzy chatter and the party atmosphere is electric, and the streets-of-Paris murals are gorgeous. In contrast, why order boring old poached eggs?'

'Mummy, that woman is talking to herself,' said a little boy, about six, at the next table.

'Hush, Simon,' said his flustered parent. 'Don't be rude, or we won't go to Hamleys Toy Shop for that Transformer robot.'

'But Granny said only crazy people talk to themselves.'

Remembering that only I could see Prill, I pulled the Dictaphone from my handbag and said, 'I was talking into this.'

Prill ignored the occupants at the adjacent table and said to me, 'Their poached eggs are sensational. It's as if they come from magic hens. And the owner's French mother bakes the bread, and they fly the amazing butter in from Brittany.'

Careful to pick up the Dictaphone as if I were talking into it, I said, 'Do the hens fly in as well?'

'Why are you asking the machine a question?' asked the precocious child as his mother blushed raspberry.

'I'm a writer dictating a story.'

'Oh, like Barbara Cartland?' the mother joined in.

I hoped not as the famous pink-clad romance novelist was in her eighties. But for ease, I said, 'Yes, except I write horror stories.'

Hopefully, that will discourage the little brat; I mean darling.

'About flying hens?' said the child.

'Oh, the car just pulled up outside,' said Mummy. 'Come on, Albert.'

An old name for such a young boy. With a relieved sigh, I watched the pair gather their belongings, leave the restaurant then step into a grey chauffeur-driven vintage Bentley.

All the other punters seemed too engrossed in chat, toast, coffee and newspapers to notice us, but I vowed to continue to use the Dictaphone as a ghost decoy.

This decadent cafe was a universe away from my usual Saturday morning experience of a sausage butty in the local greasy spoon where, after breakfast, people hopped onto buses, walked home or stepped into Ford Escorts and their ilk.

'Let's order before I point Robbie out,' said Prill.

'He's here?'

'Yes.'

'Where?'

'I need to inhale coffee before I focus on my son and his evil wife. Summon a waiter and place your order along with eggs benedict and a strong black coffee for me, please.'

'He'll think I'm a greedy pig.'

'Why care what others think? You've much to learn. Now, choose your poison, then summon that handsome young waiter with the body of a Greek god.' Prill nodded in his direction and said, 'If I were forty years younger – and alive.'

'What's the point, you can't eat it?'

'But I can sniff and admire.'

'Are you talking about the food, the coffee, or the waiter?'

'All three, darling.'

I giggled then caught the waiter's eye.

Catlike, he glided over, pulled a notepad and pen from his shirt pocket. 'What can I get you, madam?'

Embarrassed, I said, 'A pot of tea, a strong black coffee, eggs benedict, and poached eggs on toast.'

'That's a lot of eggs. What if it all gets cold? Shall I bring the poached eggs and tea first?'

How to wiggle out of this? 'If what gets cold?' I said, deliberately stupid.

He regarded me as one would a simpleton. 'Your friend's order. I presume the entire order is not for you?'

'She'll be here soon.' Gosh, I'd forgotten about my pretend friend.

'Right you are.' He grinned, then glided away.

'Gosh, that was embarrassing,' I said.

Prill grinned. 'Not for me.'

The waiter reappeared with a silver tray of tea and coffee. 'Which is yours?' he asked me.

'Pop it all on the table, please, and I'll sort it out.'

'Ah, that's delicious and could wake the dead,' said Prill, head bent over the aromatic mug of coffee. 'I feel better already.'

As I sipped perfect English Breakfast tea, I remembered the hunky man with Cruella, nodded towards them and said, 'The man with the skinny, scary woman is gorgeous.'

'Naturally, the fruit of my loins is gorgeous.'

It couldn't be. 'Your son?'

'Yes. With Stella, his evil skinny wife.'

'Why didn't you say earlier?'

'You didn't ask.'

Now I knew who the hunk reminded me of – Prill. They both had an enviable bone structure with high cheekbones and noble, straight noses as if Michelangelo carved their features.

I thought of several retorts, none of them polite, and said instead, 'Ah, here's our food.'

As I tucked into the best poached eggs and buttered toast ever, I groaned with foody bliss as Prill said, 'You sound like a 1970s porn star.'

'Sniff your eggs benedict,' I said cruelly.

'Don't be wicked; you must have taken lessons from my daughter-in-law, but I'm enjoying the sight and aroma of my coffee and food.'

Mid-chew, I glanced over at Robbie and Stella's table, where they appeared to be arguing. 'Tell me more about them, Prill.'

'Later. For now, I simply wanted to point out my son as part of our investigations. It's odd to see him without him seeing me.'

'How come I can see you and Robbie can't?'

'I have no idea.'

As a ghostly tear slid down Prill's left cheek, I said, 'It will make the investigation easier.'

'That Robbie can't see me?'

'Er, yes. Surely that makes it easy to spy.'

'I'm not that stupid, and it's not that simple,' said Prill.

That was me told.

Robbie didn't seem a killer – or even a conniver.

But I was sure Stella was both.

I glanced over at their table, and she caught my eye and gave a poisonous glare. I'd often heard the phrase 'if looks could kill,' but now it made horrible sense. What hold did scary Stella have over Robbie? I intended to find out.

Meanwhile, I had an extra breakfast to enjoy. My waistband was tight, so I vowed not to eat until dinner (or maybe breakfast the next day). Or perhaps until Christmas.

When I paid the bill, the handsome waiter winked and said, 'I like a woman who enjoys her food.'

Too mortified to reply, I nodded.

'Thanks for breakfast,' said Prill as we left the brasserie.

'Thanks for the inheritance.' Now to say what my conscience dictated. 'If we sort stuff with your son, I'm happy to give it back.'

I wasn't but had to say it or forever live with the guilt.

'Let's cross that bridge if and when we come to it, darling. Anyway, the pearl necklace I promised you is worth a tidy sum and in a safe location.'

'I thought they were faux pearls?'

'One does not advertise one is wearing a fortune around one's neck. It could lead to murder.'

I didn't point out the irony.

As we reached Newsflash, Prill said, 'Nip in and buy *Time Out*, darling, and we'll go to the pictures.'

'What's *Time Out*?'

'The best what's on in London guide.'

'Shouldn't we go home and work on the case?'

'What case?'

'Your murder.'

'Of course – silly me. But first, let's have some fun. God knows how long I'll be in this realm. Perhaps I'm only here to sort unfinished business. So there's no reason I shouldn't enjoy myself before sleuthing.'

We opted for *An Officer and a Gentleman* at the local Plaza. As Richard Gere carried Deborah Winger from the factory, I imagined Prill's son rescuing me from Feet First as Miss Harridan's mouth fell open, and Cheryl cheered. Good old Cheryl.

Near home, I said, 'It seemed cheeky only paying for one ticket at The Plaza. You could go into any cinema and watch films for free.'

'I haven't told all,' Prill said as we strolled.

'Spill.'

'Wait until we are indoors and I'm in something comfortable. This old suit is tight.'

It might have been tight but was stunning with its perfect cut. 'You can sense that?'

'Yes. As tight as when I was alive. I bought it in the sixties whilst in Paris, and I've gained weight since.'

'Perhaps imagine a larger version of it?'

'No – it was a one-off.'

'As are you. It's lovely to be with my old friend again.'

Despite the ghostly pallor, there was a slight blush on Prill's elegant face.

From my first day in Togs boutique, Prill was my fairy godmother. I was only sixteen, but she treated me with respect and, within a year, took me on a London buying trip where we stayed in the Dorchester hotel. She promised to take me to France and Italy. 'Boulogne is wonderful for cheap and fabulous clothes, darling. And Paris is divine. We'll stay in the George Cinq.'

Prill adored Mike (my boyfriend who died), and she sometimes wined and dined us in Liverpool's top restaurants when Bill, her husband, was away. Mike believed me capable of anything, as did Prill.

When Mike died, a light dulled inside me, and when I married Steve, it dimmed further.

Although I'd worked in Prill's boutique for years, she never took me on her overseas buying trips, making the excuse her husband wished to accompany her. Nor did she take me to London again. But she'd made up for it now!

But she and I knew I lost the last of my mojo, along with my zany, outrageous fashion sense, when I married Steve. Oh, I always looked smart (I hoped) but relatively safe and conservative.

An Officer and a Gentleman had a strange effect on me. Or maybe it was mere fatigue.

Back home, Prill wanted to chat, but I excused myself. 'I'm a tad tired, but will meet you in the living room at 8 pm.'

What was wrong with me? I'd wanted an adventure, but this was an adventure too far. Perhaps after seeing Deborah Winger with Richard Gere, I wished to settle down again. *No!* Not after all my dull married years.

But I wanted temporary oblivion, so I pulled off my clothes, popped on my favourite Marks and Spencer floral pyjamas and crawled under the down-filled duvet. As I pulled the comforter up to my chin, I realised my problem.

Worried about losing my inheritance to Prill's son, I'd turned money-mad within days of owning a decadent flat and a healthy bank balance. Shameful.

Viv Nicholson popped into my head – the woman who made headlines in the early 1960s after her husband won a fortune on the football pools and Viv announced she would 'spend spend spend'.

She and her husband went on a crazy shopping spree of cars, holidays, fur coats, jewellery and everything decadent but soon returned to square one.

Perhaps I was more *hoard hoard hoard* than *spend spend spend*.

But it was easier to have an exciting adventure with a plump cushion of wealth if things went awry. With this attitude, no wonder my life had been dull. Zillions of fantastic chances had probably passed by me. Without the money and posh property, would I revert to dull again?

I couldn't face another twenty years of uneventful, passion-free suburbia. Maybe that was due to the wrong partner. If Mike had lived, we'd have been happy with a small house and income. Or would we? Our short relationship never stood the test of time.

Sleep overcame me, and I dreamed I was on Oxford Street on Christmas Eve, as the Salvation Army sang 'Oh Come All Ye Faithful' outside John Lewis. An elderly woman rattled the collection tin under my nose as I said, 'My money is mine, all mine.'

I morphed into another horrible dream in which I was a female Scrooge. Nobody attended my funeral, and a dog peed on my unmarked grave.

To my relief, at 7.30 pm, the radio alarm woke me with Bucks Fizz's 'Land of Make Believe'. Ironic. Time for a quick shower before I met Prill in the living room. Anyway, due to horrible connotations, I couldn't face a bath.

I guessed Prill would be glammed-up, so I donned black velvet evening trousers and a black open-knit jumper and slipped into black mule slippers. After a hasty hair brushing, a quick slick of pale-pink lippy and a spray of Revlon's Charlie, I padded the few yards to the living room to find Prill sensational in a full-length silver silk sheath dress, white hair in a French pleat.

The mealy-mouthed attitude I'd had earlier left me. Thank God. If I had to return the inheritance, so be it. I adored Prill, always had and wanted to see justice done.

'Wow, you look sensational,' I exclaimed. 'And what is that divine exotic-garden scent?'

'It's Joyful Woman, the most expensive perfume in the world and too wonderful to be labelled *scent*.'

'Pardonnez moi,' I said with a grin. Prill's pretend snobbishness always amused me.

Prill waved a hand towards the large coffee table, which held a bottle of champagne in a silver ice-filled bucket. There were also three crystal flutes and caviar with all the trimmings – chopped eggs, crackers and toast points. 'Help yourself to Dom Perignon and a few nibbles.'

Surprised, I said, 'How did you manage it?'

A familiar voice said, 'Good evening, Milly.' Mr Crown, the solicitor, appeared as if from nowhere. Instead of his former staid pinstripe grey suit, white-on-white shirt and blue silk tie, he wore a black cloak adorned with shimmery red stars. On his head was a tall top hat. And he held a wand in his right hand.

'I didn't see you come in,' I stammered. Not sure I could cope with more paranormal stuff, I hoped Mr Crown was off to a fancy-dress party.

'A party trick of mine. Please sit, Milly.' He gestured to the sofa opposite Prill. 'Allow me to pour you a glass of bubbly.'

'Thanks.' I needed a drink.

In a daze, I sipped the ice-cold fizz and surveyed Mr Crown and Prill on the opposite sofa. They appeared very much in love, superglue-close to each other.

My chest tightened, and I nearly fainted as Peter, the opera singer, now dressed as Dracula, stepped from behind a curtain. Blood dripped from his evil pointed fangs as he glided towards me and said, 'Prepare to be undead. When I first saw you, I knew I must bite your delicious neck.'

I turned to Prill and Mr Crown for help, but their eyes flashed red as they cackled. The scene was horrific; everyone had turned against me. I didn't have a friend and wanted my old, dull life back, safe in suburbia with safe Steve.

When I noticed the coffin near a window, I went sick and dizzy, but when its lid slowly opened, and Sebastian arose from it singing 'Thriller', I woke in a cold sweat and turned off the radio alarm and Michael Jackson.

Phew.

Thank the Lord it was a dream. I could cope with Prill being a ghost – more than that would drive me insane.

I double-checked the time – 7.30 pm and, in no mood to dress up, I quickly showered, threw on a blue velour tracksuit, a spritz of lemony scent, then found Prill on a sofa in the living room. She was also in a tracksuit, but hers was Dior, not Dash.

'Are you alright, darling?' she said. 'You look like you've seen a ghost.'

'Ha flipping ha.' I told her about my nightmares as a massive chill ran through me. Maybe all this was a dream, and I still worked for Feet First; Steve hadn't gone to America, we were still married, and life was duller than dull.

It was too surreal, and I needed a drink. 'Back in a mo, Prill,' I said.

In the kitchen, I located a bottle of Valpolicella, a wine glass, a corkscrew, then hurried to the living room, flopped onto a sofa and said, 'Let's chat. We have a murder to solve.'

'We do indeed. You'll find a pen and paper in the desk drawer. Let's make a list of suspects. Do you want a snack first?'

'After what I've eaten in the last few days, absolutely not.'

According to Prill, the pen was a Montblanc, and the writing paper was antique parchment. What was wrong with good old Basildon Bond? The ornate desk was Louis XV. 'Just a little piece I picked up at Sotheby's – throw a linen cloth over it, and it doubles as a dining table,' said Prill, quaintly oblivious to her former life of privilege.

A far cry from my Fairley home furnished from MFI and Williams Furniture – *When you walk through the door your pound's worth more at Williams, where else?* The dralon three-piece-suite cost Steve and I eighty pounds in a Boxing Day sale.

Nothing in my life was normal and everyday anymore. Apart from me. I'd always felt lacklustre around Prill as if she were a goddess. But she'd never lorded it over me, had a magical aura and was a joy, even now as a ghost.

'Sure you don't want anything to eat?' said Prill.

I patted my expanding tummy. 'Positive. Although this is a holiday from normality, I don't wish to resemble a small bungalow.'

'When alive, I only ate once a day – dinner.'

'No wonder you were always so svelte. But, hang on, we often lunched together when I worked in Togs.'

'I began a few years ago when my metabolism slowed to a crawl. I discovered that constantly spiking insulin by eating little and often gains more weight than eating the same amount of calories within a shorter time. Plus, I was more alert and sharper during the day but looked forward to my one meal which tasted ambrosial whether my feast was cheese on toast or a chicken roast.'

'That rhymes.'

'What does?'

'Cheese on toast or a chicken roast.'

Hungry now on the subject of food, I added, 'If you were alive, what would you eat now?'

Prill closed her eyes and contemplated. 'A cheese omelette with a green salad followed by a few squares of dark chocolate. Or perhaps fish and chips with mushy peas, white bread and butter and a huge dollop of tartar sauce – my last meal – apart from a shortbread biscuit minutes before I died. If I'd been on death row, I couldn't have planned it better.'

I shivered. 'What a thing to say.'

'You must have thought about it.'

'About what?'

'What your last meal would be on death row.'

'No – don't be morbid.'

'Guess what Marilyn Monroe's last meal was?' Prill said.

'Caviar with champagne?'

'You're half right – spaghetti and meatballs with Dom Perignon on the side.'

'I bet that wasn't all she had on the side.'

'You naughty girl.'

'How do you know about Marilyn's last meal? Were you with her?'

'Ha-ha – I read it in a magazine.'

'Oh, I've got one,' I enthused.

'A magazine?'

'No, a famous person's last meal.'

'Go on.'

'Elvis had ice cream and chocolate-chip cookies.'

Prill and I had always enjoyed frivolous banter. As I realised how much I'd missed her, my eyes watered.

'What's the matter, darling?'

'I've missed you and am so sorry you're dead.'

Never one to brood, Prill said, 'Then let's solve my murder. Who are the main suspects?'

'The main suspect is Stella.'

'I agree. But perhaps she paid someone to do the dastardly deed.'

'That could be anyone.'

'No. Someone who lives in this building or has a key,' said Prill.

'How do you know?'

'A hunch. Besides, it's sensible to start with the more obvious suspects then spread the net wider if we fail. Illogical to begin with the entire world population then narrow it down later.'

That made sense, so I nodded as Prill said, 'Write down the obvious suspects.'

Leaning on *Vogue*, I wrote *Stella* at the top of the list and then we continued in order of level of suspicion.

Soon, the list looked like this...

1. Stella

Neither Prill nor I could imagine anyone else as the evil perpetrator.

'What about Sebastian's new boyfriend?' I ventured. 'Have you met him?'

'I glimpsed him in the hallway. He was rather ordinary to look at but I sensed an air of menace. Despite the latter, he would blend into any crowd.'

'I saw his photo and thought similar. Don't they make the best criminals?'

'Who?'

'People who blend into the crowd.'

'That makes nearly everyone a criminal.'

I giggled. 'You're awful. What's his name?'

'No idea. Just call him Whatshisname.'

'Okay. Whatshisname can be second on the list, especially as Dolly was weird about him and stuttered when Sebastian suggested he mend her boiler.'

'Dolly has good intuition.'

So, I wrote,

2. Whatshisname

Neither of us suspected Fawn, Sebastian or Peter, so they went in joint third position:

3. Fawn, Sebastian and Peter

'What about Mr Crown?' I said, 'He had keys.'

'Ah, but not until after I was dead.'

'How do you know?'

'Because I didn't give them to him when I was alive.'

'Oh, I see.' I felt rather silly. 'Are you sure you were murdered?'

'Almost one hundred per cent.'

'The post-mortem should have revealed something.'

'Perhaps the investigation wasn't thorough because of my age.'

'You weren't ninety.'

'True – but some think over seventy equals dead.'

We had five people on our list, and I thought of a sixth I hardly dared mention. Silly – as this was a murder investigation.

Luckily Prill said it before I plucked up courage. 'And, of course, we mustn't forget my son. Write his name down.'

As I did, Prill's face fell. Then she bucked up and said, 'I need a laugh. Check the television cabinet drawer and see if the *Fawlty Towers* videos are there.'

'Why wouldn't they be? Are we looking for a thief *and* a murderer?'

'No – I gave Dolly permission to borrow books and videos.'

'Should she be on our suspect list?' I said.

'No.'

'Why?'

'She just shouldn't.'

'Fair enough.' I still didn't know why her ongoing employment and wages were a condition of my inheritance. But from Prill's closed expression, this was no time to pry.

I found a *Fawlty Towers* video in a red case. 'Which episode do you want? I may have to rewind the tape.'

'Pop it in the machine, and it can start wherever.'

As skinny, long-legged Basil appeared, Prill and I laughed before he even spoke. Ironically, the episode was *The Kipper and The Corpse*, but Prill and I giggled all the way through.

'Another episode?' I said as the credits rolled.

'Not now. I want to say something. Pour yourself another glass of wine.'

The latter sentence reminded me of, 'Sit down, I have something to tell you.' The first time I experienced similar, my beloved blue budgie had fallen off his perch, and the second time Mum told me Mike was dead. I quickly recovered from Joey's demise but never got over Mike.

Prill clutched her throat, looked me in the eye and said, 'I'm a witch.'

'Don't be silly,' I said. Although maybe not so silly, as I'd always found Prill beautiful and magical.

The first time I saw her, my mouth fell open at her gorgeousness. 'You've always reminded me of Grace Kelly,' I said now.

'Oh, what a compliment – my favourite actress. Perhaps you could rent one of her movies tomorrow. And we'll watch it after I tell you more. My revelations will shock you.'

'Tell me now, or I'll lie awake worrying.'

Emulating Samantha Stevens of *Bewitched*, Prill twitched her nose, then said, 'You won't – trust me.'

After getting into bed, it was suddenly Sunday morning, and I awoke starving.

I pulled on a tracksuit and Reeboks, hot-footed it to the Great Escake and bought two large fluffy croissants, still warm from the oven. I'd have gone to Blossoms, but Fawn said it didn't open until eleven on a Sunday morning.

As I headed out of the Great Escake, Sebastian came in and said, 'I see we had the same idea. What did you buy?'

'Two gigantic croissants.'

'I'll get pains au chocolat, and we'll have breakfast together. Come to mine as the coffee is percolating.'

I half wanted to say no, eager to discover what Prill had to say, but the thought of a feast for the eyes as I ate French delights was too yummy to resist. I might explode from sensory overload.

'Brilliant,' I said. 'Sorry I look a mess.'

'Don't be ridiculous – I can't abide false modesty,' said Sebastian before mille-feuille woman asked what he wanted.

I'd always felt a mess next to gorgeous people, as I was plain and ordinary. Oh, I passed muster, but was nothing special. No wonder my marriage had been so drab. I wasn't lovely enough to light anyone's fire.

As we strolled to our building, I said, 'It wasn't false modesty. Look at me.' I tripped over a wonky paving stone as I peered down at myself, took orbit and landed on the pavement.

I thanked God for the tracksuit, which got the brunt of the fall, rather than my knees. Luckily the croissants were safe.

Recovering, I said, 'Will your boyfriend join us for breakfast?'

'No. He's gone to fix his mum's dripping kitchen tap.'

A thrill shot through me. Even though Sebastian was gay, I would enjoy a delicious time alone with this divine vision.

The pastries were gorgeous, and the coffee divine – plantations away from the Blandwell instant at home in Fairley where I didn't even own a coffee maker, just a kettle.

It wasn't only me who had lived a dull existence; my taste buds had lost out too.

'What is this coffee?' I said.

'Blue Mountain from Harrods.'

Of course – silly me. As if it would be Kwiksave's budget brand.

I doubted Sebastian had even set a calf-leather-clad foot in Kwiksave.

'How long have you known Prill?' I said.

A frown creased his alabaster forehead. 'You mean how long did I know Prill before she died?'

'Didn't I say that?'

'No. Since she moved here about six months ago. You?'

'Since I was sixteen and worked in Togs.'

'Togs?'

'Her groovy Liverpool boutique.'

'Oh, that was you?'

'What was me?'

'About a week before Prill died, we shared a bottle of wine, and she told me about a past employee who was like a daughter. But she didn't say you lacked confidence.'

If he'd said this nastily, I might have cried, but I could tell he had good intentions, so I drained my Royal Worcester bone-china coffee cup, popped it on its matching saucer and said, 'Okay, Mr Sartorial Elegance, what's wrong with me?'

On the butter-soft red leather sofa, he took my hand and looked me in the eyes. 'You are a pretty woman with a good figure but don't believe it.'

'How do you mean?'

'You wear nice clothes, albeit a tad conservative, are attractive but don't believe you look good.'

My throat closed with emotion, and I dug my nails into my hands in an effort not to cry. Nobody apart from Mike had called me attractive, apart from Prill (often), but I always thought she said it to be kind. The most positive thing Steve had said about my appearance was, 'You'll do.'

And that was on our wedding day.

As a traitorous tear slid down my cheek, followed by another, Sebastian withdrew a pink cotton-lawn handkerchief from his shirt pocket and handed it to me.

I wiped my eyes, blew my nose. 'Sorry, I'm not used to compliments.'

'So I see. However, your dark hair streaked with silver, cheeky blue eyes and slightly turned-up nose are adorable.'

He said *silver* – how lovely. I patted my head. 'I'd planned to dye it – get rid of the grey.'

'Don't you dare – you'd pay a fortune to get that effect from a bottle.'

'Thanks.'

'You're welcome.'

Chuffed to bits, I asked him to come with me to choose a kitten the following day.

'I'd love to,' he said.

Banana Studios

Sebastian called a cab on his account to take us to Knightsbridge.

A butler, white gloved and in full regalia, opened the door and said, 'Yes,' in the warm, welcoming tone of Lurch.

When I noticed the Greek statues and swimming pool in the cavernous hall, the cat got my tongue.

Bought up wealthy, Sebastian seemed unfazed by the opulence and said, 'We're here about the kittens.'

'Did you make an appointment?'

'Milly Miller for 11 am,' I said. Snobbishness usually makes me laugh, but this guy spooked me.

The butler lifted a starched cuff and glanced at his gold watch. 'You are five minutes early. Wait on the doorstep while I tell milady you're here.'

In a chilling tone, Sebastian said, 'We will not wait on the doorstep, and if you persist in the rudeness, my mother will hear about it.'

A slight flicker in the butler's eyes. 'And your mother is?'

'Lady Eleanor Luckisin.'

Golly – I'd read about her, and she was richer than the Queen.

'I will seat you in the orangery.'

BAKING AND ENTERING

An orangery and a swimming pool in central London? Before now, I had no idea such decadence existed.

'I should have brought my swimsuit,' I joked and was treated to an evil stare as Sebastian snorted.

As we enjoyed the sunny orangery, Mr Snooty arrived and said, 'Milady is indisposed, so follow me, and I'll show you the kittens.'

After we mounted an elaborate curved staircase and entered a grand drawing-room, I fell in love with the two Siamese kittens cuddled together on a blue velvet chaise longue.

'Oh, they're adorable,' I enthused.

'Take your pick – five hundred pounds apiece,' said Mr Snooty.

He'd said two hundred pounds during our phone call, but perhaps I misheard. Cute Colin cost me a fiver, and I'd had no idea pedigree cats were so expensive. How green I was.

But Sebastian pulled himself up to his full six-foot-two. 'Don't be ridiculous – the going rate is no more than one hundred and fifty pounds per cat. We will buy them both for two hundred and fifty.'

'But I only want one,' I murmured from the side of my mouth.

'Choose your favourite, and I'll have the other,' Sebastian whispered.

Mr Snooty hesitated and then said, 'Milady insists on cash.'

'I bet she does,' I muttered, guessing he would cream some off the top. As Sebastian opened his wallet, and I scrambled for my purse, the phone rang, and Mr Snooty answered.

'Yes, milady, no milady, No, not yet. We are transacting now, yes, I see. Yes, it's quite understandable.'

With an air of doom, he put down the phone. 'The kittens are no longer for sale.'

Instead of disappointment, relief flooded me as if the phone call saved me from something terrible. Strange.

On the salubrious street, Sebastian said, 'Saved by the bell – literally.'

'What do you mean?'

'I forgot Damien is allergic to cats.'

'Damien?'

'My live-in boyfriend.'

Ah, it was the first time I'd heard his name.

But why did it ring a death knell?

Ah, yes, the demonic child in the 1976 horror movie, *The Omen*. For ages after I saw it, I was scared to go to the loo in the night and was grateful I had a pleasant child without the beast's mark – 666.

Sebastian hailed another cab, and soon we were outside our building. I didn't want to go indoors as the day was sunny. 'Fancy a cappuccino?' I said.

'Sure.'

'Anywhere near with outside seating?'

'Banana Dance Studios. And it has a fab cafe.'

'How far?'

'You'll need hiking boots, it's two minutes away.'

'Done.'

At a cast-iron table outside the studio, Sebastian and I nursed chocolate-sprinkled cappuccinos and through a window observed women aerobicising in leggings, leotards and leg warmers as 'It's Raining Men' thumped from the building.

'Rather them than me,' he said. 'Although the teacher is fit – check out his rock-hard abs.'

A hardship – but I did. 'Not bad.'

'What's your husband like?' said Sebastian.

'We're divorced.'

'I know – but what drew you to him? Was it his six-pack or amazing sense of humour?'

'He's rather stout, to be honest – I'd need to dig deep to find a six-pack. Not that I can talk, my tummy needs a few million sit-ups.'

'What do you call a bodybuilder without a six-pack?'

'No idea.'

'Abnormal.'

Like teenagers, we fell about as I realised my life had lacked frivolity. Once recovered, I said, 'Steve is quite serious, doesn't usually get irony, and detests *Monty Python*. He's a custard pie kind of guy. Clowns are his thing, but they scare me. So, we mainly discussed trivia such as what to have for dinner.'

'Give me an example of him not getting irony?'

I thought hard then said, 'When we first married, I said Sunday lunch at his mother's was so fun I'd like to go every week. It took endless rubber chicken and soggy trifles to get out of it.'

'He told her your original comment?'

'Yes, and she thought it was a compliment, bless her.'

'Sounds like lack of irony is hereditary in Steve's family.'

'Yes. When I said I was suicidal because I had to work one Christmas Eve, he made a doctor's appointment.'

'For you, I presume.'

'Yes.'

'Did you cancel it?'

'I didn't know until Doctor Edwards arrived on the doorstep looking concerned. When I explained, he said his wife was like Steve, and I suggested they shack up together.'

'Did he laugh?'

'We both did. From then, we were more like mates than doctor and patient.'

'So, what are his good points?'

'The doctor's?'

'Ha-ha – your ex-husband's.'

'He's kind, reliable, never loses his temper.' *And deathly dull.*

'Fine qualities. I'm worried Damien is an unexploded bomb.'

'Damien?'

'My live-in boyfriend, the plumber.'

Oh, of course. I recalled my adverse reaction to the photograph and Prill's reaction when she saw him on the stairs.

Fear clutched my tummy, but Sebastian's sudden closed expression said he didn't wish to discuss it further. He drained his cappuccino, licked foam from his full lips, and said, 'Let's check out Old Stuff.'

'Old Stuff?'

'An antique shop in Bute Street about two minutes away.'

'Okay.'

Old Stuff was a fine emporium of beautiful objects, large and small. I spotted a lovely eight-inch-tall grey china elephant but couldn't find the price. 'How much is this?' I held the animal in the air as I addressed the proprietor, a fusty exhibit in a moth-eaten cashmere cardigan and ancient baggy trousers.

'I'll check the ledger.' He opened a large book and ran a nicotine-yellow digit down a few beautifully scribed columns. When his finger halted, he said, 'One hundred and sixty pounds and superb value. Nineteenth-century French.'

Heck! I'd imagined about ten quid having seen something similar in Woolworths. 'I'll think about it.' I'd already thought – for a nanosecond.

But Sebastian's long legs strode across the parquet floor, and he picked up the pachyderm. 'Exactly what I need for my mantelpiece. Will you take one thirty?'

Did he mean one pound thirty?

Of course not.

'Sold to the handsome gentleman for one hundred and thirty pounds. Will it be cash or cheque?' said the proprietor.

'Cash.'

Oh, of course, because everyone carried that much money around – not.

Nonchalance about large sums of money was another world. But everything is relative, I reflected – to some people, a hundred and thirty pounds was a month's rent and to a privileged cherub a mere throwaway sum.

When we left the shop, Sebastian swung the carrier bag as if it contained a loaf of bread. I was more careful with a box of eggs.

'Be careful, you'll break it,' I warned while wearing my Mum hat. As I remembered something important, I clapped a hand to my mouth. 'What day is it, Sebastian?'

'Monday all day.'

'Not Tuesday?'

'Not until tomorrow,' he said.

'What a relief.'

'Why?'

'I promised a friend I'd take her to dinner tomorrow.'

'Super. I recommend Daphne's.'

'She lives hundreds of miles away, so I'll have to travel north tomorrow.' I'd forgotten about Cheryl. How awful and self-absorbed, but I was trying to solve a murder, I justified.

Sebastian pulled a key from his Ralph Lauren blazer pocket. Opening the door, he said, 'Give her a call; you might wangle your way out of it. Want to pop in and see how the elephant looks in its new home?'

'Later – must phone my friend.'

From my living room, I phoned Feet First. Miss Harridan answered, and I said, in a Yorkshire accent, 'May I have a quick word with Cheryl?'

A massive sigh of disapproval. 'I know it's you, Milly. Make it quick as we're run off our feet since you let us down. Cheryl – your unreliable friend, Milly, is on the phone. Make it snappy.'

No way should I cancel Cheryl and confirm my unreliability. Anyway, it would be nice to see Colin.

But before I got a word in, Cheryl said, 'Thank God you called. Can we reschedule tomorrow evening? Something big has come up.'

'Cheryl, put that phone down and serve Mrs Norris with her orthopaedic sandals,' shouted Miss Harridan.

'It's fine to cancel,' I said.

'Thanks, Milly, you're a star. Must go.'

Phew – that was lucky.

While in phone mode, I called Mrs Snoops to check on Colin.

'Yes, he's fine and brought me a little present earlier – a dead mouse.'

'Oh, I'm sorry.'

'Don't be – I heard scurrying sounds and was scared, but Colin rescued me. He's a fine chap and spends a lot of time in my house, even slept in my bed last night. He wants to say hello; I'll put him on.'

Loud, contented purrs echoed down the phone.

I didn't need to worry about Colin, but maybe my daughter would have to rethink her plans to reclaim him.

As I put the phone down, Prill appeared on the opposite sofa. 'Have a good time with Sebastian, Milly?'

'Yes – great fun and lots of envious stares.'

'From men or women?'

'Both.'

'Shame about the cat.'

'About Colin, you mean?'

'Who's Colin?'

'My cat up north.'

'Oh, no. I meant the one you went to buy.'

'How did you know?'

'I was there.'

'Really? I didn't see you.'

'I can dematerialise whenever I want.'

Spooked and surprised Prill could follow me unnoticed, I rehearsed what to say, but she pre-empted me. 'I didn't plan to; it was an experiment.'

'How so?'

She explained that until we went to Banters Brasserie, her spirit couldn't leave the confines of the flat.

'Then why suggest we went if you thought you couldn't?' I knew that sounded convoluted but couldn't think how else to say it.

'A hunch and I was right. I thought Saturday might have been a fluke, so I accompanied you today and was fine. However, it appears I can leave this flat but only with you.'

I narrowed my eyes as a transparent blush shadowed Prill's ghostly visage as she said, 'I had an ulterior motive in following you. Join me for tea, and I'll explain.'

About to say, 'I just had coffee,' her anxious expression stopped me. Prill had rarely shown anxiety, dead or alive. So, I said, 'I'll make it.'

To my surprise, she said, 'Unnecessary, darling. I'll procure it.'

What did she mean?

Prill closed her eyes, waved her right hand and said, 'Fairy wings, and all things schmancy, serve tea for two most fancy.'

A doubtful giggle caught in my throat as the room filled with pink fluorescent stars as a plate of scones, a silver teapot, two china cups and saucers, two side plates, two knives, a bowl of cream, a small container of butter, and a ramekin of jam landed on the coffee table.

Overawed but sassy, I said, 'You forgot the milk.'

'Here it comes,' said Prill as a dainty milk-filled silver jug landed on the table. 'Will you serve, or shall I?'

'You.' I wondered how, as a ghost, she would manage.

But she effortlessly poured a drop of milk into each bone-china cup and topped them with tea.

With silver tongs, which appeared in her right hand, she popped a scone onto each side plate. 'Eat it while it's warm, then we'll talk.'

Dumbstruck, I did as bid, and if I'd thought the cherry scones with the exceptional Madagascan vanilla were sinfully delicious, these made them akin to shop-bought budget brands.

Nothing had ever tasted better. Not even the Smartie-covered chocolate cake Mum made for my tenth birthday.

Why was I thinking about Mum when I should question Prill?

The latter took a dainty sip of tea.

Hang on, how could Prill drink?

Could she eat too?

Yes – she piled butter, cream and strawberry jam onto a scone half, took an almighty bite and chewed.

Polite, I waited until she'd swallowed, folded my arms and said, 'Explain.'

'Not much to explain – I'm a witch, and can eat via a spell which unfortunately only lasts a few minutes.'

'But you're dead.'

'Yes, I know. Stupidly I thought my powers died with me; obviously they didn't.'

'How long have you been a witch?'

'Quite a few years.'

'Were you a witch when we met?'

'Sort of – but didn't realise until I moved to Piddleton-on-Sea. Now, shut up and let me eat.'

Somehow, I'd always known Prill had magical powers. I recalled our first meeting in 1963.

Togs Boutique

I didn't plan to leave school at sixteen, but when Dad died in the summer holidays, I sensed Mum's financial worry and decided to get a job. It wasn't entirely noble; the thought of sixth form and university did not appeal.

Unsure about leaving school, I went to Liverpool one Saturday to mooch around the shops. On a side street, I spotted Togs, a boutique, very London. Lured by 'Walk Right In' blaring from the radio and patchouli incense, I did walk right in – and fell in love. Both with the fab racks of funky and colourful clothes and the shop assistant, about fifty but fabulous, who emanated an air of magical mystique.

A stunning teenage girl, about a year younger than I, regarded herself in a white Cheval mirror. 'Is it too short, Mum?'

'With legs like those, why would you worry? Besides, you're gorgeous, and I wish I had half your looks,' I said, surprised at my outburst.

'That's what I told her,' said the mum, an older version of her attractive daughter.

'And what I was about to say.' The elegant shop assistant, a vision in a green dress I later discovered was Givenchy, winked at me.

'Okay then,' said the girl with endless legs and expressive eyes set in an incandescently beautiful face.

Was I jealous? Not a bit. What a fib – my average looks and figure could never compete.

As the assistant wrapped the dress, a slovenly girl arrived, dragging her scuffed heels, and disappeared through a door at the back of the shop.

When the mum and daughter left, the assistant addressed me. 'I'm Priscilla Hodgkin, the owner of this emporium. Want a job?'

'Where?' I said stupidly.

'Here.'

Not used to snap decisions, I again surprised myself. 'When can I start, Miss er Mrs Hodgkin?'

'Call me Prill. How about right now?'

'Fab.'

When the slovenly girl reappeared, Prill glared and said, 'Sandra, your trial is over. You'll get wages plus a week in advance.'

Obviously outraged, Sandra opened and closed her mouth. 'But it's not fair; you didn't give me a chance.'

'You had a month of chances and were tardy every morning, at least fifteen minutes late after every lunch, and rude to customers. Hardly a dream employee.'

'I'll tell my dad.'

'Oh, I'm scared.' Prill opened the cash register, pulled out three five-pound notes and handed them to tearful Sandra.

'What will I do for a job?'

'I neither know nor care, but Woolworths want someone for their broken-biscuits counter. I was tempted to apply myself, but prefer to run a successful boutique.'

'You'll be sorry.' Sandra swiftly vacated the premises.

With Prill's attitude, I wondered if I'd made a mistake. Would she soon send me packing in a similar fashion?

But she gave me a megawatt smile and said, 'Slippery Sandra was also stealing from me, but I couldn't be bothered with the drama of calling the police. Anyway, the rush will be on soon, so I'll show you the ropes.'

I wanted to buy half the shop – thanks to Mary Quant, hemlines were up, anything went, along with psychedelic colours and flamboyant patterns. Twee was out; outrageous was in. At last, people could dress to suit their personality with less worry of judgemental raised eyebrows.

As I checked the price of a gorgeous short pink shift dress, a porcine, short man stormed into the boutique on a cloud of stale sweat, waddled towards Prill, prodded her chest with a fat, filthy finger and said, 'Nobody sacks my Sandra.'

Prill looked down her aquiline nose, removed his meaty hand with a look of distaste as if disposing of dog poo, and said, 'I just did. Keep your dirty digit to yourself and get out.'

'If you don't reinstate my Sandra, I'll sue.'

'And if you don't vacate my premises immediately, I'll summon the police and tell them Sandra has sticky fingers.'

'There's no law against dirty hands. Anyway, our Sandra was brought up proper and washes her hands at least once a day.'

I suppressed a snort as Prill said, 'Sticky fingers as in *tea leaf*, you ignoramus.'

For a moment, I wondered what she meant by *tea leaf*, then remembered it was cockney rhyming slang for *thief*. Breath held, I waited for Mr Pig to explode with anger.

Face puce with outrage, he said, 'Are you offering me a cup of tea? If so, shove it; I've got pride and won't be bought.'

Prill raised a perfectly sculpted eyebrow. 'Really? Let's see about that.' Opening the till, she retrieved four ten-pound notes, proffered them, and his fat paw grabbed the notes, dropping them immediately as he screamed in pain. 'Ow, that wasp stung me.'

'What wasp?' I said.

'The one that just flew out the open window,' said Prill nonchalantly.

Mr Pig bent to pick up the fallen money, lost his balance and hit his head on the sharp corner of a table.

Howling with pain, bleeding from a deep gash on his forehead, he bravely tried to retrieve his money from the floor with his unstung hand. Simultaneously, a young woman entered the shop with a takeaway cup of tea, but she lurched forward, the Styrofoam cup flew through the air, and hot liquid drenched Mr Pig's fat tummy.

Amidst outraged squeals, he stumbled from the boutique, and his parting shot was, 'This place is a minefield, and I won't be back.'

Prill studied her French-manicured nails and said, 'Oh, what a shame.' Then she retrieved the fallen money, replaced it in the till, turned to the newcomer and said, 'Welcome to Togs. The sleeveless blue shift dress with the daisy print will be adorable on you.'

'That's what I came in for,' she said. 'I saw it in the window. Have you got a size ten?'

'Of course,' said Prill. 'It will be perfect for your friend's wedding.'

'How did you know my friend was getting married?'

'A wild guess.'

Damien Goes Crazy

'Are you recalling our first meeting, Milly?' Prill said.

'How do you know?'

'I sensed it and saw your lips twitch when you remembered Mr Pig.'

After a chuckle, I said, 'He never troubled us again, nor did his daughter.'

'No great loss. Now to tell you about my magic.'

Not sure I wanted more scary revelations, I reluctantly said, 'What sort of witch are you?'

'The good sort.'

'How do you mean?'

'My magic only works for the good.'

'How do you do it?'

'Do what?'

'Make the magic happen. Do you wiggle your nose, wave a wand or something?'

'My supreme power is karma witch, with the lesser power of kitchen witch. My other powers are more random, dependent on situations.'

'Enlighten me.'

Prill explained that if someone deserved it, she hastened their karma by wishing it. 'Mr Pig's greed hit him in the face.'

'And on the belly,' I added.

'Quite. Although I didn't realise it was magic at the time.'

'Why not wish karma upon Stella for your murder?'

'I need to know she did it.'

'But if she doesn't deserve it, nothing will happen, so why not try?'

'Spells drain magic energy, which then needs replenishment, so I don't waste them. Only when positive someone sent evil my way, do I bat it back.'

'A karmic Wimbledon?'

'Exactly.'

As I envisaged myself in a divine outfit, eating strawberries and cream at Wimbledon proper, I heard an almighty crash, a scream, raised voices, banged doors, and hammering on my door.

'See who that is,' said Prill needlessly.

Wild-eyed, Sebastian flew in. 'Damien went crazy and broke the china elephant, flung it against the wall.'

He fell onto a sofa and burst into tears.

Prill and I exchanged worried glances but let him sob.

When the sobs became hiccups, I said, 'Can I get you a drink?'

'B-b-brandy, please. That nice Armagnac.' He pointed to the drinks cabinet.

Prill grinned as if to say, 'Not so traumatised,' as I returned a complicit smile.

I poured myself a tiny tot of brandy topped with water but gave Sebastian a good healthy slug in a crystal balloon.

Handing him the drink, I sat beside him. 'Tell me what happened.'

Prill leant forwards, elegant chin in long-fingered hands.

With an attractive pout of his luscious lips, Sebastian said, 'He said I'm a spoiled brat who knows nothing of the real world.'

'That's true,' said Prill in a fond tone. 'Bless the sweet cherub child.'

Did Sebastian hear that?

It appeared not.

I waited for a few beats, then uttered the universal soothing words, 'There, there,' and patted his back – any excuse.

'I'm scared,' said Sebastian. 'Damien's eyes flashed evil as if he wanted me dead. He reminded me of a serial killer from the telly. You know, all lovely and calm before they flip. He terrified me, and I want him out of my flat.'

As my tummy knotted, I wondered if Damien killed Prill.

A timid tap at the door.

'That'll be him, don't answer it,' said Sebastian, wild-eyed again.

'It's okay; he won't do anything with us here.' Opening the door, I mentally crossed my fingers. A penitent Damien stood on the threshold. 'Is Sebastian here?'

'No.'

He ignored me, barged past, strode into the living room and held out his arms. 'Darling, please forgive me. When you told me how much the elephant cost, I was jealous.'

'No excuse to smash someone's possessions,' said Prill, apparently heard only by me.

'You scared me,' whispered Sebastian.

'It will never happen again, darling. Please come home.'

Cheek – said as if he were inviting Sebastian to his home, not the other way round.

Uncertainty flitted across Sebastian's face, but he said, 'Okay,' and followed Damien.

A lamb to the slaughter.

'What do you reckon?' I asked Prill.

'Damien is a con man. Have you seen that spooky Dirk Bogarde film, *The Servant*?'

'No.'

'It's about a seemingly humble servant who turns the tables and becomes the master. Damien is similar without the initial fake humbleness. He intends to rule Sebastian and control the purse strings, perhaps kill him once he's Sebastian's heir.'

Spooked, 'I said, 'How do you know?'

'Something in his eyes.'

Yikes. 'What can we do?'

'I'll think about it. Meanwhile, I'll tell you about my kitchen magic.'

Prill explained she could infuse food, particularly cakes, scones, biscuits and pastries, with magical powers.

'Just by thinking about it?'

'Not exactly – I make essences like the special vanilla you used.'

'But you can buy vanilla in the shops.' True, but I'd always bought budget brands.

'Of course. I usually bought mine from Harrods or a darling delicatessen in Brighton. It tasted amazing, whether magicked or not.'

'Does magic improve the taste?'

'Not always, extra butter does that, but it increases Ojalis.'

'What's that?'

'A witchy term for life energy. The more we have, the better our mood, health, and confidence. But it's not unrealistic confidence, we only aspire to what we are capable of.'

'So we don't falsely believe we can fly and leap from mountains and skyscrapers?'

'No, darling. That would be LSD. Alcohol and drugs temporarily increase our mood but soon decrease it. We are often happy after a few drinks, elated after drugs, but miserable soon after.'

'And Ojalis?'

'Temporarily boosts mood and confidence. It wears off but doesn't have the toxic effect of drugs and alcohol. Regular use of Ojalis trains the mind to be more optimistic, so eventually, it's unnecessary. That's why my cafe was such a success.'

'What cafe?'

'Baking and Entering.'

Prill was full of surprises. 'Tell me about it,' I said as she disappeared into the ether again.

Baking and Entering

When my beloved husband asked me to leave Liverpool and move to Piddelton-on-Sea in Sussex, I didn't want to leave my home town, but I'd pledged an agreement.

When he slipped the emerald and diamond engagement ring onto my finger, we agreed to live in Liverpool until I was fifty. So far in the future, I thought the time would never come. Young people never believe they will age.

On my fiftieth birthday, I expected marching orders to Sussex, but Bill accepted a plum job in Liverpool, and I got a stay of execution.

Until he took me to dinner years later and said, 'I've found us a lovely cottage in Piddleton-on-Sea.'

Luckily it was more town than village. But my husband conned me with 'cottage' using a psychological trick beloved of politicians. Threaten something 'worse', and the 'better' seems a gift or at least a reprieve.

'Cottage' terrified me with its claustrophobic connotations, and I imagined a dark and beamed building with tiny windows. So I breathed a happy sigh of relief when Bill braked his prized red Morgan on the gravelled drive of a gorgeous pale-pink villa with white columns on either side of a bright-pink front door. A large front lawn led to a wide pavement over the road from a beautiful beach.

'Do you like it, darling?'

'Love it,' I said truthfully.

'Wait until you see inside.'

The house boasted spacious light-filled rooms, and a large south-facing conservatory at the back looked across lavish tree-lined lawns.

We moved in summer, and I was happy to languish with a book on a garden lounger or carry a deck chair over to the beach, armed with a murder mystery. I loved a good whodunnit.

But one day, I realised I'd read through my book pile, so I headed to the high street and the local bookshop in search of Miss Marple or similar. And there wasn't one. A bookshop, I mean, not a Miss Marple.

Spotting custard tarts in a bakery window, I brought one each for Bill and me as a bribe for him to drive me into Brighton and bookshops. I had never learned to drive.

'That's the worst custard tart ever,' said Bill with a grimace. 'Your baking is far superior.'

I nodded and took a large glug of tea to take away the chemically oversweet taste.

'You should open a cafe,' he said. 'You can't read all day, every day.'

'No,' I said. 'I'm off to find suitable premises.'

'Now?'

'No time like the present.'

'Are you sure you don't want another boutique?'

'Been there, got the designer t-shirts.'

'Which one will you use?'

'Which what?' I said.

'Estate agent.'

'The local one – Drear and Dimley.'

Drear and Dimley had nothing suitable apart from cheerless boxlike premises in Brighton, one which had been Last Stop Funerals. Walking home along the salty-aired seafront, I noticed a cute bungalow I hadn't seen before. It appeared more retail than residential with its almost full-length windows at ground-floor level. There was no front garden, and the recessed front door opened directly onto an extra-wide pavement. Perfect for tables and chairs.

Nosily, I squinted through the glass at the usual living-room arrangement of a three-piece-suite, television, coffee table. On the coffee table in a shaft of sunlight sat a beautiful chocolate-point Siamese cat who winked at me. Winked? Probably imagination, so I rubbed my eyes, but it winked again and raised a paw as if in greeting.

As I stared, a green and gold van stopped, and a young, agile man leapt from the driver's seat, opened the hatch door and pulled out a *For Sale* sign.

'Is this property for sale?' I asked.

'Yes, but it's licensed as residential, not retail – that was the problem.'

'Problem?'

'The owner wanted to use it as a cafe and bookshop, but the council blocked all his planning applications. After repeated fruitless attempts, he left.'

'So it's vacant?'

'Since yesterday. Would you like to look around? I'm Brian Mason.'

'Prill Hodgkin. Yes, please.'

Once inside, I fell in love and envisaged what I would do with the premises – create an old-fashioned, cosy cafe within a book store dedicated to crime and mystery books. In a flash, the name came to me – Baking and Entering. A hunch told me the planning application would be a cinch.

After the recce, I said, 'Whose is the cat?'

'What cat?' said Brian.

I spotted it behind a sofa, but it shook its head and put a paw to its lips as if to warn me. Crazy. I said, 'Must have been a shadow. But I want the premises, depending on the price.' It wasn't dependent on price; I wanted (needed) it whatever the cost.

Brian named a ludicrously low figure, and I said, 'Done.'

When he went to the van to fetch his briefcase, I scooped the unprotesting cat into my wicker basket and covered it with my silk Hermes scarf.

Once the estate agent's van trundled away, the cat popped its elegant head from under the designer silk and said, 'Phew. What a close shave.'

Amazed, I pinched my arm to check I wasn't in bed asleep. No. Mouth moving like a human's, the cat said, 'It's nice to meet you.'

From the smooth voice touched with a slight huskiness – think Fenella Fielding, this was a female cat. 'What's your name? I'm Prill.'

'Saphira.' She held up a paw, and feeling rather daft, I shook it.

'But how?' I began.

Divine eyes narrowed, Saphira said, 'I'll explain once I've eaten. Do you have any smoked salmon?'

'Yes – for tonight's dinner with scrambled eggs and toast. How come you can talk?'

After a delicate yawn, Saphira said, 'How come *you* can talk? I'll explain later, but for now, I'm ravenous, haven't eaten decent food for weeks, even had to resort to cat food. The indignity!'

Despite the ludicrous situation, I laughed, popped the scarf over Saphira's head and whispered, 'Pipe down until we get home, or people will think I'm insane.' A talking cat! Whoever heard of such a thing?

After Saphira daintily ate smoked salmon served in a silver bowl, she indicated with a paw and said, 'Place a feather pillow on that armchair, then we'll chat.'

'Yes, your majesty,' I joked at her queenly air.

'How did you know I was Queen Cat?'

'Er – I didn't – just having a little fun.'

'As I was. Imagine having to endure a snobby cat such as my cousin Elvira.'

'Is she very snobby?'

'Oh, yes. Constantly boasts about her catestry.'

'Catestry?'

'Yes – cat ancestry. Now, about that pillow.'

'I'll get it.' Besides, I wanted to locate Bill.

I dashed upstairs to our bedroom, where my husband was reading *The Times*. Except when I glanced again, it was *The Witching Times*.

What on earth?

He removed his spectacles, lowered the newspaper and said, 'Is Saphira here?'

Bemused, I said, 'Er – yes. I've come to get her a feather pillow. What on earth is going on, Bill?'

'I'll come downstairs with you, let Saphira explain.'

Now, years later, I needed to explain to Milly. How to do it? Just jump in, I guessed. The words would come to me I hoped. It was time to reappear in my London living room, now Milly's London living room.

Birthday Party

After a while, Prill reappeared. I had many questions but began with, 'What's the real reason you followed me to Knightsbridge, Prill?'

'To check that I could leave home without you.'

Arms folded, I said, 'You hardly ever lie, but you glance downwards first when you do. Like when you lied about the handsome stranger.'

Prill organised a fabulous bash for my twenty-first at Liverpool's Adolpho Hotel. It was terrific but slightly marred by Steve's jealousy, which was strange as he never usually suffered from the green-eyed monster.

As I popped a mini asparagus quiche and salad onto a plate, I looked across the room and saw a beautiful young man hand Prill a fat envelope. Our eyes met (mine and his) as a hormone-charged lust beam shot through my pupils down to my toes.

Overwhelmed, as I had never experienced anything like it, even with Mike, the shock petrified me as Steve said, 'Who the hell was that?'

'No idea.' I wanted to run after the dark-haired vision of delicious manhood – not practical due to my three-inch stilettos, tight dress, and newly married status.

Lips pursed, Steve said, 'He wanted to ravage you on the dance floor.'

Oh, how lovely. 'Don't be daft; I'm a married woman. Let's find a table and eat our food because the quiche looks and smells gorgeous. Besides, I've never known you to be jealous before.'

'I'm protecting my new wife.'

'That's nice,' I said.

'Hang on a mo. I'll grab one of those green boats with prawns in. What are they do you think?'

'The little sign says avocado prawn,' I observed.

'What's an avocado when it's at home?'

'No idea. But I'll get one, too.'

We loved the new flavour and moaned in unison.

That was as sensual as my twenty-first birthday (or most days) got. After more savoury food, then generous slices of moist and tasty birthday cake, Steve refused to dance, and I knew he was still sulking about the tall, dark and handsome stranger. He wouldn't even dance to his favourite – 'Hi Ho Silver Lining'. His eyes followed me everywhere, even to the loo, so I didn't get a chance to ask Prill who the handsome chap was.

Even Mum said, 'Did you see that delicious man, Milly?'

The next day I woke up with a champagne hangover and dragged myself to Togs, where Prill made me a strong cup of coffee and handed me a sausage sandwich. 'Sorry you have to work today, darling.'

'No worries, I love busy Saturdays.' After three fortifying sips of Maxwell House instant coffee and a massive bite of sandwich, I said, 'Who was that handsome man last night?'

She cleared her throat. 'There were lots of handsome men at the party.'

'This one was a God – tall, slim with dark curly hair and a body for sin.'

'Oh, I don't recall.'

'But he handed you an envelope.'

Prill looked downwards. 'Did he? I have no recollection due to too much bubbly.'

After Prill's generosity, it seemed churlish to pursue the issue, so I polished off my sandwich and prepared for a busy day.

Thinking back, he was like a young version of Prill's son.

A bolt of lightning hit me.

Books and Bites

'Prill?'

'Your tone sounded ominous.'

'I've put two and two together.'

'Clever of you. Did it make five?'

'Ha, flipping ha. It's about your son.'

'What about him?'

'I reckon he was the handsome man at my twenty-first.'

Prill buried her head in her hands. 'It's time I revealed all. I'm not being rude, but try not to interrupt as my life is, or was, complicated.'

'Mine wasn't until recently.'

After a wry grin, Prill said, 'That's partly the problem.'

'My dull former life?'

'Sort of as I don't want to overwhelm you with too much too soon.'

'How much more overwhelming can it be? My best friend is a ghost.'

Prill reddened as tears filled her eyes. 'I'm your best friend?'

'Of course.'

Not a slushy person usually, I surprised myself when I said, 'You're a best friend and second Mum rolled into one.' Since Mum married an American and moved to Florida when I was thirty, I missed her.

'Thanks, darling. Now, where do I begin?'

'Start with the craziest and work down.'

Prill barked with laughter. 'You asked for it, so I'll start with Saphira, the talking cat.'

'Sounds like a Disney movie.'

'If Walt were alive, I'd sell him the rights for a fortune.'

'You'd have to be alive also,' I couldn't resist.

'Thanks for rubbing it in.'

'Sorry.' But I couldn't wait for Prill's revelations and, like a child at bedtime, said, 'Tell me everything.'

'Okay, but you asked for it.'

I sat spellbound as Prill told the tale.

Saphira, a familiar, about two hundred years old, had graced the lives of many good witches and warlocks. When an evil vampire bought the Piddleton-on-Sea premises, intending to call it Books and Bites, Saphira put many obstacles in his way, and the premises became Prill's business – Baking and Entering.

'It took three years for the WFGC to oust him,' said Prill. 'And all the while, poor Saphira was stuck there.'

'What's WFGC?' I asked.

'The Witches for Good Council,' said Prill. 'The *W* stands for both witches and warlocks.'

'Is there a WFBC?' I said.

'Witches for bad?'

'Yes.'

'Of course. The eternal fight of good versus evil. I have a horrid hunch that Damien, Stella and possibly Peter are from the dark side.'

'And Sebastian?'

'A sweet innocent who could easily be turned.'

Many questions flooded my brain.

'Your brow is furrowed, darling,' said Prill.

'I'm confused.'

'What flummoxes you most?'

'Does everyone have the potential to be a witch or warlock?'

'Only those who have lived at least nine human lifetimes.'

'How can you tell?'

'With the Spiralameter.'

'What's that?'

Prill pursed her lips, paused a while as if in thought. 'You know how you can tell the age of trees?'

'Yes – by rings in the trunk.'

'Well, a Spiralameter can tell how many lifetimes someone has lived by the rings around their pupils.'

'Eye pupils?'

'Yes. The rings are only visible to the naked eye of top witches and warlocks or to any witch or warlock who uses a Spiralameter.'

'What does a Spiralameter look like?'

'A mini magnifying glass. There's one in the desk drawer.'

'Oh, can I try it out on myself?'

'No need, darling. You're not a witch.'

I wasn't sure whether to be disappointed or relieved. 'When did you discover you were a witch?' I said.

'When Saphira the cat told me.'

I thought back to the day I first met Prill. 'You must have known about the karma thing. I mean, what about the day you sorted out Mr Pig?'

'There were many such instances, darling, but until Saphira told of my magical powers, I put it down to coincidences.'

'Hey, where is Saphira?' I said.

'Ah, we have come full circle. Saphira is the reason I followed you to Knightsbridge as I could not let you buy a kitten.'

'Why not?'

'Because I want you to adopt Saphira, currently trapped at Paws Pets' Home in Battersea. Her soul visited me earlier and purred for help. Poor thing, I've been worried sick about her.'

'How will I know her?'

'She's insanely beautiful, will take your breath away, and will be the only Siamese cat on the premises. You must rescue her tomorrow.'

'But...'

'No more buts, darling. I am off to join my husband in Saint Tropez for a romantic night. I'll tell you about him another time – but he's magic in more ways than one.'

Dizziness descended as a strong hunch hit me. 'You're not dead, are you Prill?'

'As dead as when we first met.'

'You were a ghost even then?'

'Yes.'

Shortbread

I couldn't cope. How had I worked for a ghost and not known?

Tentacles of terror tightened around my tummy, and I needed to wake because this had to be a dream.

'Milly, darling,' said Prill in a soft voice. 'Everything is alright – you only fainted.'

Woozy, I said, 'It was a shock to discover you were already dead when I met you.'

'Who told you that?'

'You did.'

'Not true – I've only been dead since last month. You fainted after I said that Bill was magic in more ways than one.'

Fear hugged me in its awful grasp as I shivered. 'I can't cope with these awful dreams and visions.'

Sat on the floor beside me, Prill said, 'Tell me.'

I regaled the awful dreams in which Peter was a vampire, Sebastian rose from a coffin and all the other horrors.

'Did you see colour in these dreams?'

'Yes.'

'Was there a fragrance?'

'Why, yes, a powerful scent of vanilla.'

Prill clapped silently. 'By Jove, I think I have it.'

Despite my fear, I smiled. 'You sound like Professor Higgins in *My Fair Lady*.'

'Similar, darling, as you are my protegee.'

''Ere, are you sayin' I don't talk proper?'

'Your ability to form a proper sentence and not talk in grunts and slang was part of my immediate attraction to you. I needed a dictionary to understand Sandra.'

'I wonder if she took your advice,' I mused.

'What advice?'

'The job on Woolworths' broken biscuits counter.'

'I believe she started a charm school.'

'You're kidding!'

'Naturally. Now, onto the sofa, and I'll tell you more if you're up to it.'

I wasn't but nodded, did as bid.

Once settled with Prill beside me, she said, 'The Madagascan vanilla may help find my murderer.'

She explained that in the wrong hands the magic essence could cause people to have visions which drove them crazy with fear and open to suggestion. 'And I reckon someone stole two bottles.'

'Are you sure?'

'Absolutely – which they used on me to ill effect.'

'How come?'

Pain crossed Prill's lovely face. 'When I returned from Crown and Scimitar on the day of my death, I was overset and desperate for a cup of sweet tea and a biscuit.'

Ah, the British answer to every trauma. 'I get it – go on.'

'I kept homemade shortbread in a tartan tin in the larder.'

Bile rose in my throat. 'Is there more than one tartan tin?'

'No.'

'Oh dear.'

'What?'

'I ate a few.' Thinking back, I snaffled two before my nightmares and one before my most recent faint.

'Did you buy or bake them yourself?' said Prill.

'No. I presumed Dolly put them there.'

'Are there any left?'

'One or two.'

'Fetch the tin and let me sniff.'

I retrieved the tin, removed the lid and held it under Prill's nose.

'Pick up a crumb, hold it directly under my nostrils,' she said.

I did.

With a grimace, she said, 'I sense black magic.'

The only 'Black Magic' I'd encountered were the chocolates of the same name. 'What does that mean?' I said.

'A dark witch or warlock could say a spell when baking with my magic vanilla and change its essence and intent. For good, the magic vanilla increases Ojalis, but for bad, it has the opposite effect. It makes people doubt their abilities, have no faith in their intuition and wish to sabotage everything good in their lives. A mere whisper of evil when under the influence can have disastrous effects. Even cause someone to commit suicide.'

Every hair on my body stood on end, and I turned stone cold. Prill and I stared at each other and said, 'Oh, my God.'

'Murder by vanilla,' said Prill.

Perhaps the Death by Chocolate Cake craze was less innocent than it appeared. I dared say the unsayable, 'Prill, might you have drowned yourself?'

'A distinct possibility. I must put the jigsaw together.' She clicked her fingers. 'I just remembered Saphira wasn't here when I returned from Crown and Scimitar. Whoever baked the fresh batch of shortbread probably stole her, and they could only do that by doctoring her smoked salmon as it was the only thing she would eat without numerous sniffs and pokes of a suspicious paw.'

'You still haven't told me about your son.'

'All in good time, darling.'

Drat – I needed to know.

Before I turned off the bedside light, I set the radio alarm for 8 am and checked the *London A-Z* for the location of Paws Pets' Home in Battersea. Imagining Colin's wrath, if he ever discovered I'd replaced him, I fell into a fitful sleep and woke to a strangely high-pitched Freddie Mercury singing 'I Want to Break Free'.

Although I loved the song (and Freddie), I was more in the mood for Mozart, so I turned off the alarm, but Freddie carried on singing.

Then I realised it wasn't the radio but a voice inside the flat. I popped on my dressing gown, slipped into my slippers and shuffled into the living room to find Dolly hoovering away as she segued into 'My Baby Takes the Morning Train'.

It was nice to see someone so happy in her work. Like Miss Harridan. Not.

'Good morning!' I shouted, but she was oblivious, so I pressed the off button on the vacuum cleaner as, on a cloud of musky rose perfume, Dolly swung around. 'Good morning, ducks.'

'You're early,' I said, realising this was nonsensical as I had no idea what her regular hours were.

'Early? It's past nine. Did I wake you?'

'Luckily,' I began, 'because the radio alarm didn't go off, and I have an appointment.'

'That thing's temperamental – like me.' She laughed, then burst into racking coughs, pulled a floral hanky from her floral pinafore and coughed into it. Now a tad queasy, I was desperate for a cuppa.

'Join me for a cup of tea?' I said.

'Lovely, ducks, but I'll make it while you get dressed. Fancy a slice of toast?'

'Yes, please.'

I hurriedly had a cat's lick at the bathroom sink, threw on linen trousers and a lightweight sweater and dashed to the living room where Dolly awaited.

'I popped your brekkers on that side table, ducks.' With a pink-taloned hand, she pointed to a teetering toast mountain and a mug of tea.

'Thanks,' I said. 'It's nice to have the chance to chat.'

'Absolutely, ducks. A little bird said you inherited this place?'

'Oh, yes?'

I wasn't sure how much Dolly knew or why I had to keep employing her – not that I minded – and wondered why Prill had been so secretive. But if I let Dolly talk, she'd probably spill many bags of beans.

'Aren't you having toast, Dolly?' I said to avoid her inheritance question.

'No, ducks. I had a massive cooked breakfast. But don't mind me – scoff away.'

'Thanks. Tell me about yourself while I do.'

She did – with no idea Prill was next to her grinning away.

Apparently, Dolly had only known Prill for a few months. 'I started working for her when she moved into this place, and she was good to me. I used to be a right misery, but the sun came out the first day I worked here and hasn't gone back in again. All my life, I was unlucky until I met her, but I'm right sad she's gone.'

'So am I,' I said, between bites.

'I was here the day she died.'

'Really?'

'Yes – she wouldn't have known as I got a last-minute dental appointment which clashed with the Thursday I was supposed to work, so I came here the day before, the Wednesday like, and the next day I found she'd died – tragic – such a lovely woman and so beautiful. Taught me to make the most of myself, she did.'

Greedily on the third slice of toast, I said, 'Really?'

'Oh, yes. I had mousy, straggly hair, wore no makeup, and my clothes were dreary and stuffy – crimplene trousers with elasticated waists, nylon blouses, all that guff and all in horrible colours. And look at me now.'

She stood up, removed her pinafore and gave me a twirl reminiscent of an older Anthea Redfern in *Bruce Forsyth's Generation Game – Give us a twirl, Anthea*.

'Gosh – you look fabulous,' I said. 'That orange and pink floral-print dress is heavenly. Is it silk?'

'Genuine imitation silk,' she said proudly. 'I got it from the market, but it looks like the real thing, doesn't it?'

'It does.'

Concern crossed her brightly made-up face. 'You don't think these earrings are too big?'

I observed the disc-shaped pink earrings, the size of dustbin lids. 'No, they're perfect.'

The entire ensemble, from the pink diamante pins in her bouffant blonde hair to the pink wedge shoes, was perfect for this larger-than-life likeable character. She had a childlike innocence and sense of fun, but I also discovered astuteness when she said, 'I don't trust Sebastian's boyfriend – a nasty piece of work.'

'How so?' I was trying to be a tad Miss Marplish.

'Shifty eyes, close together. Wouldn't trust him an inch.'

'Because of his shifty eyes?'

'Not just that – I found him rooting in a cupboard when I came to clean on the day Prill died. "Oy, what are you doing here?" I said. "How did you get in?" Now, I don't talk like that to decent folks, but he rubbed me up the wrong way from the word go.'

'And what *was* he doing here?'

'Dunno. But he said the flat door was ajar, and he was checking Prill's cat was okay. Liar liar pants on fire. Plus, that beautiful cat disappeared the day Prill died. And I don't entirely trust that opera singer geezer either.'

The plot thickened. 'Why?'

'A hunch. Pavarotti talks about his ex-girlfriend, but I reckon he's hiding something horrible.'

Pavarotti? Oh, of course – Peter.

Curiouser and curiouser.

I glanced at my watch. 'Thanks for the toast, Dolly, but I'll love you and leave you.'

'That's what all the men said, ducks, before I met Prill. Now they love me and never want to leave – the saucy sods.'

With a grin, I fetched my outdoors accoutrements, not forgetting my *London A-Z*.

On the stairs, I met Peter, who said, 'Can you feed my fish this afternoon?'

'Not until at least 2 pm.' I wanted plenty of time to organise the cat rescue.

'That's fine, as I won't be back until this evening. You'll find the key under the mat and fish-feeding instructions by the tank. Cheers.'

Paws

I wondered why it was important to feed fish to such a rigid schedule. But what did I know about tropical fish? At least, I presumed they were tropical and complicated, not common goldfish, a typical fairground prize. Not many lucky fish survived incarceration in a water-filled plastic bag after being awarded to winners at coconuts shies, rifle ranges, etc. Mine, Jules Verne, survived about a day. 'Waste of time buying that bowl,' said Dad. But he bought me a replacement fish, Jules 2, which lasted two weeks.

This was no time to contemplate fish; I had a talking magic cat to collect. A cab with a 'for hire' light appeared; I raised a hand, it halted inches from the curb, and I hopped in.

'Where to, love?'

'Paws Pets' Home.'

'That's funny. I collected my last fare from there.'

'Today?'

'Yes – just dropped her off in Chelsea.'

A frisson of fearful intuition made me say, 'A slim woman with a pointy face?'

'Yes, love, and a nasty attitude. Didn't even leave a tip.'

It had to be Stella. 'Did she have a pet with her?'

'Yes. A cat in a basket.'

He made it sound like chicken in a basket, that popular 1970s pub meal and I tried not to laugh whilst I worried the cat was Saphira. 'Did you see it?' I said.

'The cat?'

No, the Leaning Tower of Pisa. 'Yes.'

'No, but as I turned onto King's Road she screamed and nearly made me crash. "What's the matter, lady?" I asked her.'

'And what was the matter?'

'She said she left Paws with a beautiful Siamese cat and it had just turned into a mangy one-eyed brown moggie. I should have dropped her at the loonie bin. What a nutter. I'm worried about that cat, me being an animal lover. She didn't seem the type to be kind to animals – had a mean mouth.'

'Do you have pets?' I said to be polite and to oil the wheels of what I was about to ask.

'Yes – rats and tarantulas.'

Revolted, I said, 'Oh, lovely.'

He banged the steering wheel and guffawed. 'I'll say this for you, love; you've got bottle to react so calmly. The missus and I have chihuahuas.'

Now he was jesting by going to the other extreme. 'You're pulling my leg.'

'No, I'm not. Hang about.' He ferreted in the glove compartment, pulled out a framed photo. 'Check that out – the missus with Blake, Alexis and me.'

'Such a cute photo,' I said as I admired the cabbie, his wife and two cute miniature dogs – one with a pink hair ribbon, one with a blue. It was the dogs with the hair ribbons, not the cabbie and his wife.

'We love our babies to bits,' he said tearfully.

While he was misty-eyed, it was time to pounce. 'Could you tell me exactly where you dropped the skinny woman and the cat?' I said. 'A friend works for the RSPCA, and I'll get her to check the poor animal.'

'Alright, love, as you've got an honest face, and it's about animal welfare, but I could lose my licence for giving out such info, so don't land me in it.'

'Wouldn't dream of it.'

'66 Sidmouth Street, Chelsea.'

Prill had told me that her son and Stella lived in Clapham, so what was she doing in Sidmouth Street? *I must find out.*

But first, I had an exotic cat to rescue. And if I did save Saphira, would she turn into a one-eyed moggie on the way home?

'I'd like to adopt a cat, please,' I said at Paws' front desk.

An ample-breasted friendly woman who emanated the aroma of Eau de Damp Dog said, 'Have you had cats before?'

'Since I was six.'

Eyeing my empty hands, she said, 'Is the cat carrier in your car?'

Drat – I'd forgotten about taking Saphira home in normal-cat fashion. From Prill's description, she'd be happier in a kitty sedan chair. 'Oh, sorry. I forgot.'

Her eyes narrowed. 'Not a good start – being forgetful. What if you forget to feed it?'

'If she's anything like my Colin, it would be impossible to forget.'

'Is Colin your husband?'

'No, my cat.'

'Ah, so you want a friend for Colin?'

The formerly friendly woman had morphed into a Gestapo interrogator, and I needed to show adequate emotion fast.

With a tissue pulled from my shoulder bag, I dabbed my eyes. 'Colin is my daughter's cat, and she took him to her new home. He's so sweet with fluffy brown fur and great big trusting eyes. I don't know what I'll do without him.' Suddenly, the tears were genuine as I would miss that cheeky boy.

All doubt left her face. 'I'll show you the cats, and you can choose one reminiscent of Colin.'

To pave the way for my Siamese choice, I said, 'Perhaps I need one that looks entirely different – move on, so to speak.'

'That's the ticket, pet.'

Halfway down the second aisle of cat cages – so sad – there was Saphira, regal despite her basic surroundings.

'Oh, I love her,' I said truthfully. She was the platinum blonde version of Elizabeth Taylor as Cleopatra – in short, a knockout.

'How do you know it's female?'

'She's so pretty,' I said.

'I know – but it was awful when we found her on the doorstep on the brink of death. I was as if something had sucked the energy from her.'

I shuddered. 'How awful.'

'Yes. But Pyewacket usually hisses at potential adopters, puts them off, but she's purring at you.'

'Pyewacket?'

'Yes – I named her after the cat in *Bell, Book and Candle*, that film about the beautiful witch who married Jimmy Stewart. I initially wanted Pyewacket, but whenever I picked her up, she clawed me. Look.' She rolled up her sleeve and showed me some angry scratch marks.

'Ouch. May I take her today?' I ventured.

'Yes, why not? She obviously likes you. Get your basket from the car while I prepare the adoption forms.'

Remembering I lied about the cat carrier, I continued the charade. 'Back in a mo.'

I lurked outside for a suitable amount of time, returned indoors and said, 'Oh, dear. I left the hatchback open, and the basket is missing.'

'Tut tut. What is the world coming to? We have a few carriers for sale, but they are quite pricey.'

'No problem. I'm happy to support such a wonderful cause.'

On the way home in a cab, Saphira behaved as any typical cat would on a journey – wailed and whined, and didn't speak an intelligible word. Had I got the wrong cat? Surely not.

Talk about Hollywood moments. As soon as we were in the flat and I opened the cat-carrier door, Saphira leapt like a greyhound from its trap, sprang into Prill's arms, and they covered each other with kisses. I could almost hear violins and smell the syrup. But it was lovely.

To let them catch up, I said, 'I'm off to feed Peter's fish.'

'Has he any salmon in the tank?' said Saphira. 'I'm hungry for something tasty.'

Until then, I hadn't believed she could talk.

'I'll nip to the fishmongers in Bute Street, get you some smoked salmon,' I said.

'And a few prawns,' shouted Saphira as I closed the door.

BAKING AND ENTERING 109

In Peter's flat, the complicated fish-feeding instructions amazed me. A pinch of this, a peck of that – *Peter Piper picked a peck of pickled pepper*. Somehow clumsy with trepidation, I dropped a small brown glass bottle, and it rolled under the table which held the elaborate tank.

On my knees, I stretched my arm and retrieved a bottle of Madagascan vanilla.

The hair at the nape of my neck stood to attention. Could Peter be Prill's killer?

A creak on the stairs. A key in the lock. Footsteps.

I stood immobile as the living-room door creaked open, and Peter appeared – with a knife.

How I wished I was safe at home with safe Steve.

'What have you there?' said Peter in a menacing tone.

I backed away. 'More to the point, what are you doing with that knife?'

'It's a letter opener. I always open my post after rehearsal because if I see a big bill beforehand, the worry spoils my voice.'

Phew.

Still unsure he didn't plan to kill me, I said, 'You're early.'

'The soprano had a sore throat, so we postponed rehearsal until tomorrow. What's that in *your* hand?'

'Vanilla. I found it by the fish tank.'

He slapped a hand to his forehead. 'That's where it went. About a week before Prill died, I told her I'd lost my confidence, and she gave me that bottle, said to put a drop in my coffee whenever I needed a boost. Sounded daft, but I didn't want to upset the old dear.'

Not sure he was telling the truth, I wanted to flee. 'I fed your fish. Now I'm going shopping.'

'Where to?'

'Kensington High Street,' I improvised.

'I'll give you a lift as I forgot to pick up my dry cleaning from Pressed and Perfect.'

I wanted to refuse, but it might have seemed strange and ungrateful. 'Okay.' Surely he couldn't murder me in the car.

Or could he?

As Peter parked his maroon Austin Princess on a Kensington side road, he nearly crashed into a parking meter, and his hands were shaking.

'Are you okay?' I said nervously.

He shook his head. 'I saw a ghost.'

Had Prill followed us? 'Where?'

'There.' He gestured with his head as he slunk down in the seat. 'It's my ex-girlfriend with her mum.'

Across the road was Stella...

with Mr Crown's assistant.

Dropping Eaves

I had to follow them, but how to lose Peter?

Think fast, Milly. I had it...

'You're in shock, Peter. Shall I collect your dry cleaning?'

'Sure you don't mind?'

'Not at all.'

'I want to go home.'

'Good idea – give me the dry-cleaning ticket.'

He took forever to find his wallet and fish out the ticket, which I grabbed rather rudely. Shame on me, but I was in a desperate hurry.

With a frantic glance, I noticed my targets nearing the end of the road.

As they turned right onto Kensington High Street, I was about twenty yards short of the road end.

Short of breath, with a painful stitch, I turned the corner, but they had gone.

But at least I knew where Stella's mum worked and the Sidmouth Street address.

Pausing to catch my breath, I peered along the crowded pavement, and as a tall couple moved towards a zebra crossing and cleared my view, the targets entered Barkers of Kensington, and I sped onwards.

'Hey, look where you're going,' said a young woman in a lurid yellow dress.

'Sorry,' I shouted over my shoulder.

When I entered Barkers, Stella and her mum were studying a store map beside a hat display. Worried either might recognise me, I put on a straw boater, pulled the large brim over my eyes.

'The Garden Cafe is on the third floor, Mum,' Stella said. 'Let's have tea and sandwiches, then visit the dress department.'

'Good idea.'

'The escalator is over there.'

'Lead on MacDuff,' said Stella's mum.

I dashed to the nearest cashpoint, bought the hat, then rode the escalators to the Garden Cafe.

Luckily it was busy, so my sleuthing should not be too obvious. My targets were at the front of the queue, and I was behind three elderly ladies who couldn't decide between fresh-cream chocolate eclairs, Victoria sponge, rock cakes, ginger cake, and coconut cheesecake.

'Get on with it,' I muttered.

One lady sensed my impatience. 'Go in front, dear. We are such ditherers.'

'Are you sure?' Gosh, that sounded like I asked if she was sure they were ditherers.

As I was about to amend the question, she said. 'Of course – go ahead.'

'Thanks very much.'

Catching the assistant's eye, I said, 'A cup of tea, please.'

'Anything with it?'

'No thanks.'

After a disapproving tut, she said, 'Until 3 pm, you must have something with it.'

To hasten proceedings, I chose the first thing I noticed in the chill cabinet. 'A chocolate eclair, please.'

'Hey, it's the last one,' said the woman who'd let me jump the queue. 'Some reward for doing a favour.'

'Sorry,' I mumbled and, in a louder voice, addressed the assistant. 'I've changed my mind – Battenburg cake, please.'

'I should think so,' said the woman behind me.

For once, I didn't care what I ate or drank; I only wanted to eavesdrop.

Once I paid, there was another obstacle. My targets were at the table nearest the lingerie department, and tables within eavesdrop distance were occupied. I dawdled across the cafe, hoping for a miracle.

A lady at a perfectly placed table glanced at her watch and proclaimed, 'Look at the time, Joyce. We'll be late.'

Joyce shrieked, and they gathered their belongings while I hovered as my heart thumped.

When they left, I sat, pushed their cups, saucers and plates to one side, removed my items from the tray, all the time with the hat's brim over my eyes. My targets had barely begun their snacks as they were engrossed in whispered chatter. And they seemed oblivious to me.

Steve always said I had ears like a bat, and that afternoon it came in handy.

After endless dreary talk of cleaning products and ironing techniques, Stella said, 'I can't take much more of of the latest target, Mum. He's more boring than Peter and a horrible kisser. Can't we retire to the Caymans with our favourite men and what's in our Swiss bank accounts?'

'No, petal. Because the Peter con fell through, we must make up the shortfall. Meanwhile, you can always see Damien in Sidmouth Street when he pops over to 'mend a dripping tap'.

Sebastian's Damien? Surely not. And was the 'latest target' Robbie or someone else? Or perhaps Robbie was the main man and Damien Stella's 'bit on the side'. But it couldn't be Sebastian's Damien as he was gay. Or maybe he was bi.

I ate my multi-coloured cake one tiny nibble at a time, eager to glean more.

As I reached the marzipan, the chatter dulled again.

'Is that a new blouse, Mum?'

'I've had it for years.'

'How do you keep it so white?'

'I never do a mixed wash and always pop a drop of lemon juice in the rinse water.'

Gosh, this was like panning for gold – a valuable nugget, then endless rubbish.

'What will you and Dad have for dinner tonight?' said Stella.

'Steak and kidney pie – that reminds me, I must buy potatoes on the way home.'

Yawn. Who knew criminals were so dull? But they couldn't discuss their marks, wheelings and dealings all the time. Even Bonnie and Clyde had to do laundry and plan meals before they met their horrible end.

But my sleuthing was worthwhile when Stella said, 'I'm bothered Robbie hasn't heard his mum's will yet.'

'Some daft but complicated clause Priscilla Hodgkin wanted. It's a pity she only rented her London flat but you'll still get the Piddleton-on-Sea house and a wad of money.'

Ha – little did they know. Mr Crown had done a thorough job. 'I suppose, Mum.'

'No *suppose* about it – you and your man will be very happy.'

'I love him, Mum. He has dark and magical powers, and sometimes his eyes flash red – it's so devilish and exciting.'

Was she talking about Robbie, Damien or someone else?

'You were always drawn to the dark side, petal. You pretended your favourite doll was Marie Antoinette, chopped her head off, and used ketchup for blood. Your poor cousin had nightmares for months.'

With a rictus grin, Stella said, 'It nearly killed her. On the subject of death, it was lucky Prill drowned and let my man off the hook. Or so he says. Although I wish he felt guilty as I do.'

'What are you guilty about, petal?'

'Tampering with Robbie's first wife's car brakes.'

Mum put a gentle hand on Stella's arm. 'Petal, you're innocent – you paid someone to do it.'

Aha – so that was how criminals justified dastardly deeds. What a crock.

'Thanks for easing my conscience, Mum. As my beloved says, it's unfair that some people have all the dosh. He's a marvellous modern-day Robin Hood, on a quest to make life fair.'

'So you don't believe Priscilla Hodgkin's death was accidental, petal?'

'No – I believe my beloved murdered her, but I don't know how. I'd love to know, so I have something on him. You were so lucky to get that job, Mum. All those rich people to target, based on their last wills and testaments. But my first target was horrific – it was yucky sleeping with an octogenarian, even for a few nights. The thought of his saggy bottom makes me ill, and as for his saggy...'

'Don't finish that sentence, petal. But the experience was surely worth the money?'

Stella pouted. 'I suppose. Another time, I had to pretend to be a lesbian to get the money from that actress. Actually, that was rather fun, but why is it always me?'

'Because you're younger and more desirable than I. Besides, I've taken lots of risks, all that snooping in Crown and Scimitar in the dead of night. Mr Crown is secretive, incorruptible, and files estates worth over a hundred thousand pounds out of my view. It's a pity Peter renounced his inheritance before you married him as he was about to hit the jackpot.'

'Too noble by far, but I suppose that saved his bacon. He said life is more fun when he has to work for money.'

'Stupid man,' said Mum.

'Oh, look. My beloved is heading this way,' said Stella, eyes shining.

I looked across the room, expecting to see Prill's son.

But it was Damien. Sebastian's Damien.

Every hair on my body prickled.

I couldn't wait to tell Prill what I'd seen and heard.

Perhaps her son was an innocent victim, as it seemed Peter was.

As I hurtled upstairs to my flat, I bumped into Peter on his way down.

'Ah, you remembered my dry cleaning.'

'Of course.'

I handed it over as he said, 'I'll pop it in my car – it's my Don Giovanni outfit for dress rehearsal.'

Although desperate to see Prill, I needed to make up for my earlier brusqueness. 'Feeling better?'

'Yes, thanks. It probably seems silly, a man my size behaving like a big girl's blouse, but that woman had a terrible effect on me.'

'I'm a good listener if you ever want to talk.'

'I'd love that. Are you free this evening?'

'Yes – pop down for drinks at eight.'

'Perfect. I'll bring the dry-cleaning money. How much was it?'

'The price is on the bag.'

The dry cleaning wasn't the only message I'd remembered. As I entered the flat, Saphira shouted, 'Did you remember my smoked salmon?' before I reached the living room. Gosh, she was more impatient than Colin, who usually greeted me before he demanded food.

In the living room, I said, 'Would you like it on a silver platter, your majesty?'

'No – on the antique willow-pattern plate.'

Alongside Saphira on a sofa, Prill said, 'She's not joking. I bet no other cat eats from priceless china.'

'But I am no ordinary cat. When I've eaten, I'll tell you what I did to Stella this morning. So comical.'

'You mean substituting yourself with a one-eyed moggie?' I said.

From her elevated position on a high cushion atop the sofa, Saphira said, 'You know about that?'

'Yes. How did you manage it?

'I'll tell you after my smoked salmon.'

I dropped into a low curtsy and said, 'As you wish, your majesty.'

Resplendent in a purple Jean Muir creation, Prill said, 'At last, Saphira

meets her match. About time.'

The elegant cat winked and batted her with a playful paw as I giggled, headed for the kitchen. Tempted to pop the smoked salmon in a plain bowl as a joke, I thought better of it and located the antique plate, terrified of dropping it.

Saphira was sassy but fun, and I liked her. Thank God.

With a slap of her thigh, Prill said, 'Oh, but that's hilarious. You made the one-eyed moggy look like you?'

'Yes. That spell only lasted about an hour, but my timing was perfect. How dare that awful woman try and steal me?'

'How did you know it was safe to come with me, Saphira?' I said.

Oriental eyes narrowed, she said, 'Due to my supersonic powers of extra-sensory cat perception honed over two hundred years. I experienced the same positive energy as when I first saw darling Prill. I also know the one-eyed cat has won the heart of the elderly lady who lives at 64 Sidmouth Street.'

My chest expanded with relief. 'Are you sure?'

'Absolutely. Right now, the lady is feeding Precious plump and fat prawns from Marks and Spencer.'

'Precious?'

'That's the cat's new name. Precious has landed on her paws.'

'Don't cats always?' I joked.

'I suppose we do – felines rule the world.'

Such modesty – but she wasn't wrong.

Prill smiled as she stroked Saphira's head. 'Tell Milly your background.'

Although desperate to regale the day's experiences, instinct said I should let Saphira go first, as when I glanced into her stunning turquoise eyes, I saw the wisdom of the universe. 'Please do, Saphira.'

She licked her lips. 'Although always beautiful, I lived nine lives as a normal cat without special powers. But each time I escaped death, I became more perceptive. After my ninth life, when I nearly drowned, I developed superpowers, and after that, whatever happened to me, I survived and am now immortal, or whatever the cat version is.'

'Imcatal,' I said.

'Cat Goddess?' suggested Prill.

'Yes – that will do. Call me Cat-Goddess Saphira. Now, where was I? Oh, yes – whenever I use too much energy fighting evil, I become almost powerless while I recuperate.'

'The poor darling was exhausted when I rescued her from the proposed Books and Bites before I turned it into Baking and Entering.'

'I miss the sea air,' sighed Saphira. 'London is dreadful for my complexion.'

Prill rolled her eyes. 'You don't have a complexion, darling.'

Saphira waved a dismissive paw. 'Don't split cat hairs – you know what I mean.'

Behind Saphira's back Prill winked. 'Of course, darling. Now, tell Milly about that vampire you were stuck with for a while.'

Recalling a nightmare, I hugged myself.

'What's the matter, Milly?' said Prill.

'The awful dream when Peter was a vampire with fangs.'

'Peter, who lives here?' said Saphira.

'Yes.'

'Oh, how funny.' She laughed so much she fell from her cushion, onto the sofa, and onto the floor.

'What's so funny?' I said.

Back on her exalted throne, Saphira said, 'Peter is too nice to be a vampire.'

This didn't correlate with my vampire knowledge. 'But what if someone bit him and turned him into one?'

'One what?'

'A vampire.'

'You've read too many novels, seen too much television. Those are imaginary vampires. True vampires are energy suckers, not bloodsuckers. The most accomplished ones can suck enough life force from a person (or cat) to cause death. And trying to conquer or thwart them is enervating,' said Saphira.

This vampire talk was a fang too far for me, and Prill sensed it. 'Enough about vampires, as I believe Milly has important news.'

I threw her a grateful glance and said, 'I saw Stella earlier and guess who she was with?'

'Who?' Prill and Saphira said in unison.

After a theatrical pause, I said, 'Mr Crown's assistant.'

Prill's eyes widened. 'Never! How do they know each other?'

'According to Peter, she is Stella's mother.'

Prill gasped. 'Tell us everything.'

I regaled my sleuth experience up to before Damien appeared, then said, 'You'll never guess who appeared next?'

'Father Christmas?' said Saphira.

'Oh, get on with it. I'm on tent hooks,' said Prill.

I grinned at her use of the malapropism the Togs handyman had used whenever nervous about a bet. He was crazy for the horses.

'Cat got your tongue?' said Saphira.

'This needs a drumroll,' I said.

Saphira managed a long and loud purr in its stead, after which I announced, 'Damien.'

A shocked silence as the news sank in, but Prill was first to speak. 'I probably know what happened. Give me time to think.'

'Oh, there's something else to add to your thinking pot,' I said.

'What's that, darling?'

I told Prill about the bottle of vanilla in Peter's flat, and she slapped her forehead. 'Silly me – I'd forgotten that.'

'Are you sure you didn't give any others away?'

'Definitely not.'

Maths has never been my best subject, but I was okay with the basics. 'So, only one bottle of vanilla is missing?'

'And I'm almost certain who took it. Come on, Saphira, let's leave Milly to rest while we put our heads together. We'll love you and leave you, Milly, and reconvene tomorrow morning. Do you have plans for this evening?'

'Yes – Peter is coming for drinks at 8 pm.'

'Have a lovely time, darling. And you'll find a bottle of Stolichnaya under the frozen peas. Peter loves his vodka.'

With that, Prill picked up Saphira as they both began to dematerialise.

'Where are you going?' I said, feeling like Cinderella.

'Off to solve my murder. Don't feel abandoned, as I have a feeling Peter will supply a vital piece of the jigsaw.'

Peter

Peter was most appreciative of the vodka. 'I got used to it on a trip to Russia, where we performed *Queen of Spades* by Pyotr Tchaikovsky. Marvellous experience, marvellous.'

'Did you enjoy Russia?' I said.

'Very much. Things are more difficult there.'

Baffled, I said, 'And that's why you enjoyed it?'

'Yes, because it's a challenge. If a light bulb blows in London, I nip to Peter Jones and buy a new one. But in Russia, the task can take a day or more.'

I recalled black and white photographs of bread queues in 1914 Russia and compared it to a nip to the Great Escake in 1987 London. 'And that's good? To search for a light bulb?' *Not my idea of fun.*

'Of course, more of an achievement. When life is too easy, we don't appreciate it.'

I realised why he gave his fortune away but was still curious. Sneakily I said, 'Another shot?'

He held out his glass. 'Churlish not to.'

I joined him for companionship, but on average downed one shot for every three of his. Still, I became a tad tipsy.

Because of the drink, I dared say, 'Why did your ex-girlfriend spook you so much today?'

His nostrils flared, and I worried he might slam down his glass and storm out, but he said, 'She's my ex-fiancée and an evil scheming witch.'

Gosh – he had her to a tee. 'What was she scheming about?'

'My inheritance.'

I didn't mean to say it, but it slipped from my mouth: 'Before I collected your dry cleaning, I nipped to Barkers for a quick snack, and your ex and her Mum sat next to me.' *Well, it was only a little lie.*

'Did you hear anything interesting?'

'Yes.'

He raised his eyebrows. 'Do tell.'

'Perhaps I shouldn't.'

'Come on – you've started now.'

I hate alcohol's tongue loosening qualities. Would it upset Peter if I told the truth? His avid gaze upon me, I said, 'She was disappointed you refused your fortune.'

He closed his eyes and covered his mouth, and I worried he was upset. But his body began to shake with laughter. Recovering, he said, 'Ah, my dastardly plan worked.'

'What plan?'

'I felt trapped with Stella, worried she was a dangerous nutcase who would do anything for money.'

I tried to appear nonchalant. 'And?'

'Well, I turned thirty-five recently and was about to inherit a fortune.'

'Did someone die?'

'My grandad – ten years ago.'

'So, how come...'

'Grandad thought twenty-five was too young to inherit a million pounds, so it was supposed to hit my bank account on my thirty-fifth birthday. So my trustees and I instructed Mr Crown, my solicitor, to make it my forty-fifth birthday.'

The penny dropped. 'And Stella didn't want to wait that long?'

'No, that's what confirmed she wanted my money. She didn't leave me straight away, tried to make it look as if money didn't matter. However, she tried to persuade me to reverse the decision, but I said it was a done deal, triple-signed by my trustees.'

'And is it?'

'No – but don't tell her that. Mr Crown is a clever man.'

It wasn't the first time I'd heard that. 'Did Mr Crown's assistant know it was reversible?'

'I doubt it. My trustees are cautious. We transacted the business in Dunthornes and told Mr Crown to keep the documents at home.'

'Dunthornes?'

'A gentlemen-only club in Soho. Three ex-wives fleeced my main trustee who now trusts no woman.'

Swallowing a gulp of laughter, I said, 'And you're over Stella now?'

'Just about. At first, I was upset she only wanted me for my money. But she might have bumped me off to get at my dosh.'

No might about it.

'When I saw Stella earlier, all my self-doubt flooded back. But when I got home, I popped a few drops of that special vanilla into my coffee as Prill instructed. Since then, I can't imagine what I ever saw in her.'

'Prill?'

'No, you silly – Stella.'

Stifling a yawn, from tiredness, not boredom, I had one last question, 'So you're definitely over her?'

He placed a hand on his chest, and I thought he would burst into song. 'I'm grateful I escaped, maybe with my life. She bewitched me originally, but I'm furious with myself.'

'Why?'

'For falling for her in the first place. Still, it was a lucky escape.'

Cheekily, I couldn't resist saying, 'So will you give all your money away?'

'Why would I?'

'To move to Russia and live simply.'

He slapped a muscular thigh and barked with laughter. 'It's okay to have romantic notions when you know you can escape poverty by phoning the bank manager. But I'm sure the real thing is horrendous.'

Thank God he was human, after all, as he'd made me feel guilty about my inheritance joy. 'One for the road?'

'Hell, yes.' He picked up the vodka bottle.

When Peter left, I meandered to bed, and as the room span from too much vodka, I hazily reflected that it was maybe a waste for me to live in London. Even the idea of a hectic social life tired me. Perhaps I was a home bird after all, and Steve had been the perfect partner. Then I recalled the surge of passion that shot through me when I saw Robbie, Prill's son, in Banters Brasserie.

In a sober corner of my mind, I knew my thoughts were incoherent but continued my divine Robbie fantasy,

I imagined us cosily snuggled on the sofa in the evenings. And in bed at nights – and maybe during the days. So perhaps I should settle down with someone gorgeous – namely Robbie. Or was it the alcohol speaking? After all, I'd only been in London a few days and was busy solving a probable murder. Imagining Robbie in bed with me, I passionately kissed the pillow and, as if fifteen, said, 'Oh, Robbie, I love you.'

Even in the dark and under the duvet, my face burned with embarrassment. What if Prill heard me? What was wrong with me?

I never had, and I mean never, fantasised about Steve. George Harrison, yes – but never Steve. I recalled what a friend said once. 'It's time to move on when you imagine your partner with someone else and not have one tinge of jealousy.'

To confirm this, I imagined Steve doing a horizontal dance with various people.

My mother – yuk. *Get that vile image from your head right now, Milly.*

Miss Harridan? I guffawed in the dark.

Cheryl? Gosh, I could imagine that quite nicely – so vivid I felt like a dirty voyeur. Yikes.

I quickly stopped that salacious line of thought and instead thought of Colin as my eyes filled with tears. I would be jealous of whoever got him, even my daughter – he was such an affable cat.

What did that remind me of? Oh, yes, that game where you go through the alphabet with adjectives for the parson's cat.

The parson's cat is an adorable cat.

The parson's cat is a beautiful cat.

Or maybe negative adjectives.

The parson's cat is a cunning cat.

The parson's cat is a demonic cat

As I reached *demonic*, I thought of Damien, shuddered and returned to positive adjectives.

At *fabulous*, my mind blurred then it was morning and 9 am.

A Quick Trip

In the living room, I flicked through T*ime Out* as I waited for Prill and Saphira. Not surprisingly, there were endless things to do in London. Once this murder malarkey was over, I would start with the Victoria and Albert Museum, only a short walk away. But after years and years pining for London, I wasn't as excited as I ought to be.

Perhaps Piddleton-on-Sea would be more suited to me, and it would be so lovely to live in a cute seaside village, yet near Brighton for shopping.

Gosh – how ungrateful – already wishing for something other than my fabulous London flat. Maybe because I hadn't dared desire much in the years between marriage and divorce, I was in hankering overdrive. Or perhaps I should be careful what I wished for.

But Piddleton-on-Sea *would* be the best of both worlds, and the summers on the south coast heavenly. And with a big enough garden and a quiet road, I could keep Colin. But what if he and Saphira didn't get on?

It was silly to worry about things that hadn't happened – but that was the definition of anxiety. According to Cheryl, anxiety was worry about the future, and depression was despair about the past. Had I fallen into the trap of thinking all fear of the future would disappear with a fat bank balance? And why did I have this awful free-floating anxiety? Could it be because I ate poisoned shortbread?

The solution seemed obvious – put a drop or two of the positive-vibes vanilla into a cup of coffee.

No, I wouldn't risk it; who knew what Damien or whoever had done? Best to wait until Prill and Saphira's return.

But perhaps I'd sell the London flat and move to Piddleton-on-Sea. But why even dream of Piddleton-on-Sea? Apart from a family holiday in Brighton during the freakishly hot summer of 1976, I knew little of Sussex.

Brighton had been one of my favourite holidays ever, but I put that down to wall-to-wall sunshine and unputdownable books such as *The Thorn Birds, The Boys from Brazil* and *Salem's Lot.*

But perhaps there was more to it as I hadn't wanted to leave and cried on the way home.

As a spooky memory emerged, my skin prickled. Whilst in Brighton, I nipped into town to buy a bikini for Kaye's birthday. 'One of those with the cute skirt, Mum.'

As I left Young Miss, a gipsy woman approached me and said, 'You're not from these parts, but one day a magical force will draw you to Piddleton-on-Sea. Cross my hand with silver, and I'll tell you more.'

'No thanks – I must get back to my husband and daughter, but here's something for your trouble.' Lest she cursed me, I gave her a shiny fifty-pence coin. But how odd. Now I wished she'd told my fortune. Or was it just a coincidence about Piddleton-on-Sea?

'You're miles away,' said Prill, suddenly in the room.

Forcing myself to the present, I said, 'Sorry. What happened? You seem half happy, half sad.'

'Astute of you, darling. We paid a little visit to Sidmouth Street last night. I hovered outside while Saphira slinked through a downstairs window.'

'66 Sidmouth Street?' I stated the obvious.

'Yes. And I'm both relieved and angry.'

The relief had to be from good news. 'Tell me the good news first.'

In a tearful voice, Prill said, 'They didn't mention Robbie, so perhaps he never planned to kill me.'

I clapped. 'Oh, fantastic.' *Did Robbie and I have a future after all?* I'd felt guilty imagining myself in bed with a possible murderer.

'And the bad news?'

'Damien murdered me,' said Prill.

My blood turned icy as I clutched my throat. 'So, it *was* murder?'

'Yes – not accidental death, thank God – I mean, who drowns in the bath? It's such a cliché, darling.'

'So Stella is innocent?'

'Only of that, but guilty of several other crimes. Stella and Damien, not to mention her mother, are demonic. I have lots to tell you.'

Probably in for the long haul, I said, 'Fancy a coffee?'

'Not here. I want to escape this place as it feels like a tomb. Let's all visit my favourite cafe via a small detour.'

'What cafe? What detour?'

Prill touched her nose. 'Wait and see.'

'And who is all?'

'Me, you and Saphira.'

I groaned.

'What's the matter?' said Prill.

'I'll be the nutter talking to herself again, and whoever heard of a cat in a cafe?'

'This is no ordinary cafe, and Saphira is no ordinary cat,' said Prill.

'Where is it?' I asked.

'Not saying – it's a surprise.'

'How will we get there?'

'Float.'

'I can't float.'

'Darling, don't be a doubting Thomasina and trust. When you married Steve, all your magic and wonder disappeared, and you depended on logic.'

I wanted to object, but it was true. Before Steve, I had magical dreams.

'Ah, here's Saphira now,' said Prill. 'Shall we go?'

'I'll fetch my coat.'

'No need, darling. Close your eyes and trust.'

In moments, I was a feather in a strong gust of wind which became a tornado. Round and round I spun, weightless, and with a gentle thud, landed on something foamy and luxurious. I sniffed a fresh but salty fragrance. Sea air?

'Open your eyes,' said Prill.

Slowly I opened my eyes to find myself on a sumptuous gold sofa in a large and airy living room. An enormous window with gold silk drapes framed a gorgeous view of the sea and pebbled beach across a wide road.

'What do you think?' said Prill.

'Is this Sussex?'

'Yes. Piddleton-on-Sea.'

'Your old house?'

'Yes.'

Weird – but I'd come home.

Oh, I know I said that about London, but this was where the real me belonged.

'Welcome home, Milly,' said Saphira.

Swallowing a large lump in my throat, I said. 'What did you both discover last night?'

'Hear me out, then we'll visit the cafe,' said Prill.

Saphira yawned. 'Last night was so taxing. I'm going to sleep on my favourite bed.' She bounded from the sofa and onto the floor, then gracefully padded away.

Prill leant back and crossed her long, slim legs. Glam as ever, she was in a fitted white skirt suit with a black and white polka-dot blouse with a pussycat bow. I'd never look that good alive, never mind dead.

'Come on, Prill, I'm on tent hooks.'

She laughed and said, 'Okay, I'll dive right in. I was never a fan of long denouements in mystery novels, so I'll cut to the chase.'

'That's a long way of saying you'll cut to the chase,' I teased. 'Get on with it. Let's have the gory details.'

Without further preamble, she said, 'A few days before my murder, Damien broke into the flat and purloined a bottle of my magic vanilla. Access was relatively easy due to Stella having a key to the main building due to her liaisons with Peter. We must change the front-door lock.'

'I'll organise it tomorrow,' I said. 'Go on...'

'Back in Sidmouth Street, he made a batch of shortbread and added a few drops of it as he incanted, 'Eye of newt and fin of trout, let's snuff this old lady out...'

Indignant, I interrupted. 'Were you supposed to be the old lady?'

'Well, I am, or was, darling.'

I harrumphed. 'Seventy-four going on gorgeous.'

She patted her hair, neat in a French pleat. 'Thanks, darling, but that's by the by. Stop interrupting, or I'll never finish.'

With a lip-zip motion, I said, 'Sorry.'

'Now, where was I?'

'Damien's spell.'

'Oh yes – it went like this...'

Eye of newt and fin of trout
   Let's snuff this old lady out
   When she consumes this poison most vile
   She will herself revile
   And whatever her former ways
   Will feel the need to end her days
   When she gets into the bath
   She'll drown herself to end the wrath

It was a terrible rhyme, and despite the seriousness of the situation, I snorted.

'I'm glad you find my death so humorous,' said Prill.

At first, I thought she was serious and dug my fingernails into my hands to stop laughing, but when Prill winked, all was well.

'How do you know this?' I said.

'Saphira said that Damien, Stella, and her mum were at a scrubbed-pine kitchen table in Sidmouth Street celebrating their cleverness with spaghetti Bolognese, green salad, and a few bottles of Chianti. Their tongues couldn't have been looser, each outboasting the other.'

I thought of a flaw in Damien's plan. 'How did he know you would eat the poisoned shortbread?'

'Simple – he boasted about that also. On the day of my death, he entered my flat, emptied the original biscuits from the tartan tin, put the poisoned ones in their place, and said a spell as he waved a wand.'

'Do wands work?'

'Pah. They are merely silly props for egotistical wicked witches and warlocks.'

'Can you remember the second spell?'

'Unfortunately, yes. It will be engraved on my soul for eternity.'

'Is it as bad as the other?'

'Shakespeare would not fear competition.'

Prill treated even serious stuff with humour, unlike some who put a negative slant on everything, even trips to the supermarket. With Prill, most things, apart from the death and illness of others, were treated with a light touch so as not to depress people. An admirable quality.

But in this case, was her confident attitude a cover for despair?

'Do you remember drowning?' I said.

'I didn't – but it came back to me when Saphira told me what she overheard.'

Poise left Prill as she dropped her chin to her chest and covered her eyes. 'How could I let it happen? I watched it happen, watched me abuse myself but couldn't stop. It was awful...'

Prill Recalls

When I got home after changing my will, I was devastated, as any mother would be. I was almost sure Robbie wouldn't harm me, but doubt nagged. Besides, I could not let Stella access my fortune, as who knew what evil she would do? Perhaps even kill Robbie to get at his inheritance.

The next day I would call Barry Brillo, the detective chap my friend recommended. His sleuthing saved her life and fortune and earned her husband ten years in a white-collar prison. Ironic, as I was in a similar situation with my son.

I'd always done my best for Robbie, but he had a gambling addiction. Even at school he took bets on how many times the maths teacher said, 'Are you with me?' during a lesson.

When Milly saw Robbie at her twenty-first, he was returning the money he stole from my dressing-table drawer. It was to pay for Milly's party, but he planned to spend it at the Grand National on a horse called Great Lark. At the end of her tether, his current girlfriend told me. I phoned Robbie, said if he did not return the money by the end of the evening, I would call the police. And I meant it.

As an aside, Red Alligator won the Grand National that year and Great Lark was a non-finisher.

Anyway, if you threaten something and don't mean it deep down, the other person knows it's meaningless. Idle threats are useless. A genuine threat delivered in a soft voice is infinitely more powerful than a loud, empty threat.

Despite my many former empty threats towards Robbie, this time I meant it from the depths of my soul. He had spoiled my otherwise perfect life with Bill.

I saw the white-hot glance between him and Milly, and it terrified me. The poor girl was still hurting from losing Mike, was freshly married to Steve, and I didn't want her hurt again or stuck with a gambler.

But what if all along, Milly had been who my son needed?

And vice versa?

Not that anyone should need anyone, we should live our lives dependent on nobody – a good relationship being the icing on a well-baked cake.

Because however scrumptious the icing, it can't make a lousy cake taste good.

But who was I to talk? I've always had Bill…

aka Mr Crown of Crown and Scimitar Solicitors.

How to unravel the confusing mess and explain it to Milly? It would be easier to take her to the cafe, hope she fell in love with it and go from there.

And Saphira, if not in a sassy mood, might help.

But I was forever haunted by the day I died and became a ghost.

When I got home from Crown and Scimitar, I needed someone, or some cat, who understood, so I called Saphira but couldn't locate her. In the fridge, I checked for her smoked salmon, and it was gone. Strange. She usually waited for me to serve it on her special plate, which she made me buy from a Sotheby's auction.

What a cat.

A cup of Lapsang Souchong and a shortbread biscuit would help, so I fetched both and settled on the bed to enjoy them. Usually, about three nibbles into one of my special biscuits, my mood lifted, but this time it worsened.

Worried and dejected, I ran a hot rose-scented bubble bath and lay back in its steamy depths. That didn't help either. A heavy black cloud descended and pushed me under the water. It wasn't just my imagination, and I had to force myself to the surface. My throat tightened as if my throat chakra was suffocating me. I'd had enough of this life; the next would be easier, I reasoned, so I gave in to the black cloud and let it push me under without a fight.

It was terrifying, claustrophobic, but then euphoria enveloped me, and I looked forward to sweet oblivion, the release of all worry.

I let myself go and welcomed the sweet bliss.

When I saw Milly in the flat, I thought it was a dream. But I knew I was a ghost when I tried to touch her, and my hand was formless.

Although dead, my mind worked fast, and I realised she was my heir due to the changed will, and that was why she was in my (her) flat.

But where was Saphira?

I called endlessly – *Saphira, Saphira,* but she didn't come. Usually, my magic muse would be there instantaneously.

The day before Milly rescued her, I heard Saphira's sassy voice as if from a deep tunnel. 'Help me, Prill. I'm trapped in Paws Pets'

Home and don't have the energy to escape. Someone poisoned my smoked salmon.'

Now, I had to explain all this to Milly.

But first, I'd take her to Baking and Entering.

Floating

'Come on,' said Prill. 'It's time to visit the cafe.'

'Is Saphira coming?'

'No – she has a task to do.'

'What task?'

'I'll tell you later.'

'Will we float there?' I said.

'It's the only way to travel.'

'It beats British Rail. Could I travel-float unaided?'

'No. I must accompany you.'

When we floated through the cafe door in a puff of pink smoke, none of the well-dressed punters seemed to notice.

Prill and I landed on a plush red chair apiece on either side of a round rosewood table. On it was a tiered bone-china stand laden with cakes and sandwiches, a teapot, cups, saucers, all the accoutrements.

I'd expected Baking and Entering to be closed with no edibles available. However, it was a hive of activity and rife with aesthetically pleasing sights, joyous sounds and divine appetite-teasing aromas.

The cosy but elegant cafe buzzed with merry chatter and the clink of silver against china.

On the three walls not occupied by the counter filled with culinary delights were shelves groaning with books. It was a cake and book lover's paradise.

All I needed to complete it was Robbie.

Why couldn't I get him out of my mind? It was as if we were destined. *Don't be silly, Milly, you've watched too many romantic films.*

'Do you like it?' said Prill.

'Love it, but I'm too nervous and excited to eat. I thought the cafe was closed?'

'It is.' Prill picked up a pink iced fancy.

'Then how come...?'

'This is your imagination. We're in the London flat.'

'And Saphira?'

'Resting after an important mission.'

As Prill snapped her fingers, the cafe disappeared, and I was in the London living room.

'Saphira is asleep on your bed – get used to it as I don't want her to leave your side for a few months once I'm gone.'

'Gone?'

'If Saphira's mission was successful, my work here is done.'

Tears filled my eyes. 'You're not leaving me?'

'Only to spend more time with my husband. However, I'll visit you from time to time.'

But her husband was dead, wasn't he? As was Prill. To think I'd once thought Alice in Wonderland farfetched. 'Please explain.'

'Later – here's Saphira looking smug. Did it work, Saphira?'

The Siamese slinked across the carpet and hopped onto a sofa as if weightless. 'The three of them are in the car now, and you can activate the instant karma spell.'

'What car?' I said.

'The car of doom,' said Prill. 'I'll perform the spell then tell you more.'

She stood, raised her hands to the heavens and said,

Eye of newt
And tongue of frog
I must do this
It is my job
You did not repent your evil ways
So you cannot be one who stays
You killed my son's wife
And many more
Now you must die
That is natural law
Your karma I now on you exact
You can't escape
And that's a fact
Imminny shimminy central beam
With all my heart this spell, I mean
Let justice be done
You've had your fun

Prill waved her hand as thousands of multi-coloured moonbeams and angel wings radiated from it, then she fell onto the nearest sofa and said, 'Thy will be done. Let the guilty die and the innocent survive.'

She lay motionless awhile, and I worried she had died – again. Impossible – ghosts couldn't die twice.

Could they?

And that awful karma poem would score zero out of ten in a poetry class, so surely it achieved nothing.

'Is Prill okay?' I asked Saphira.

She stopped licking her snowy-white back to stare into my eyes. 'Give her a few minutes. That was a powerful spell.'

'It didn't sound powerful.'

Saphira smirked. 'Ah, you judged it by literary merit of which it had none. Big mistake – huge.'

'What should I judge it on?'

'The intention behind the words. Humans are silly and judge the outer world more than they should. What matters is souls and their intentions.'

A cat was lecturing me – albeit a 200-year-old talking cat. On second thoughts, maybe Saphira had more wisdom in one paw than I had in my entire body. Not difficult.

A groan.

'She's coming around,' said Saphira.

'Are you okay, Prill?' I said.

Prill sat up slowly, blinked several times. 'Wow, that was powerful. I hope it worked.'

Nonchalantly, Saphira studied a paw. 'Karma is now in charge – and will punish the guilty accordingly.'

'How?' I said.

'Wait and see. I'm going to lie down. Do you mind if I use your bedroom, Milly?' said Prill.

As if I would say no. 'Of course.'

'When I'm rested, I'll tell you some possibilities, and you may choose your future.'

'But...' I began, but Saphira shook her head and put a paw to her lips as Prill left the room in a half float, half stumble.

'I thought ghosts didn't need sleep?' I said.

'Witch ghosts do after karma spells – the most exhausting of all. Also, it's rather problematic,' said Saphira.

'Why?'

'Because if the spell-sayer misjudged the supposed evil-doer or doers, the spell bounces back at them.'

Worried, my tummy churned. 'Surely Prill has no bad karma to bite her nose.'

'True – but the WFGC could take privileges away.'

'Such as?'

'She might have to wait a few years to spend time with her husband.'

'But he's dead.'

'Didn't she tell you the story?'

'Not entirely.'

'Then it's not for me to say.'

Saphira was contrary – and a mind reader.

'You think I'm contrary,' she said.

'No, I don't.'

'Liar liar pants on fire.'

'Well, maybe a bit. Can't you fill in the gaps of what Prill hasn't told me?'

'Prill's story is not mine to tell. But mine is. Ask away.'

'Tell me your story,' I said.

'Are you sitting comfortably?'

Saphira Reminisces

I was born in Siam in 1787. When I was a kitten, six-year-old Princess Apinya adopted me, and her father, the king, said I was the most pampered cat in the land.

Princess Apinya, a well-intentioned sweet child, dressed me in doll clothes and draped heavy jewels around my neck so I could barely move. To my embarrassment, she pushed me about the palace and its grounds in a pram.

Intuitive from an early age, I knew what side my salmon was buttered, so I endured these humiliations during daytime.

But by night, I crept from Princess Apinya's bed and became a real cat – caught mice, raided the kitchen and pushed valuable vases to the floor where they smashed to smithereens.

When I was fourteen and Princess Apinya was twenty, and about to marry, I'd lived eight of my nine lives and was worried about dying for good as I didn't wish to leave Apinya. Her father had affianced her to a rich old man, Prince Nimkon Poop, who Apinya hated. 'Oh, he's ancient, and he smells, Prija.' Prija was my name at the time. 'I don't wish to marry him. And guess what?'

Then, I couldn't talk but gave a questioning glance touched with sympathy – I'd seen too many scrawny cats outside the palace grounds to be ungrateful of my pampered circumstances.

Being a cat, I didn't make my gratitude too obvious – a cat-code acceptable level of snootiness must be adhered to at all times.

You may have noticed that cats seem aloof – true – but that aloofness is painted with brilliance – we show enough occasional affection, so you still love us but don't feel secure in that love. *Keep them guessing* is the international cat motto.

Now, where did I get to?

Oh yes. Princess Apinya did not wish to marry Prince Nimkon Poop. Also, I discovered he was jealous when Princess Apinya lavished affection on me.

'Why not stroke me instead of that stupid cat?' he spat one day.

The answer was clear – I was beautiful, and he was a pockmarked ancient with sagging jowls, colossal eye bags and bad breath.

Due to the many mirrors and clear lakes and ponds dotted in and around the palace, I knew I was a great beauty, even in the cat world.

One night, Prince Nimkon Poop collared me during my nocturnal wanderings and threw me in the ornamental lake as he said, 'Ha, that will get rid of you, vile feline.'

Gasping with shock, I swallowed a mouthful of water, went dizzy and lost hope. But perhaps there would be lots of lovely salmon in the great cat home in the sky.

But I didn't want to die, so as life slipped away, I prayed to Bastet, the fabled cat goddess. 'Oh, Basted, rescue me from this watery grave, and I will serve you all my days.'

A potent force lifted me from the water and deposited me at the muddy lakeside, where I coughed up a giant furball and three small fish.

After a short while, the king's dog, a brown Ridgeback, sat beside me and licked my fur as he said, 'Get on my back, and I'll take you to Princess Apinya's bedchamber.'

Was this a dream, or had I died? 'You can talk?' I said without thinking.

'So can you, it seems.'

Well, how about that? A talking dog.

The next day, exhausted, I slept on Princess Apinya's bed all morning. At noon, she appeared and said, 'I'm lunching with Prince Nimkon Poop today, and he wants to bring the wedding forward, but I would rather die. Oh, Prija, you must do something. Last night I dreamed you were a magic cat and gave my future husband a repulse of me, and I married a beautiful young man instead, and we had three children. What's more, I dreamed you, my best friend, could talk.'

She'd called me her best friend – flattering even for a cat, although the cat code forbade me to show too much appreciation.

But I had to save my princess. Besides, I didn't want to be trapped with Prince Nimkon Poop either.

It seemed I could also read. I recalled a particular book in the library and visualised the spine, which said *Spells for Witches and Familiars*.

It was now or never. 'Bring me the large red-bound book from the library entitled *Spells for Witches and Familiars*.'

Princess Apinya's eyes widened. 'Oh, Prija, you can talk. The witch said you could, but I didn't believe her.'

'What witch?'

She clapped a hand to her mouth. 'I wasn't supposed to tell anyone lest Sunee loses her job.'

'Sunee?'

'Yes, the cake maker. She said she's a good witch, and I have the potential to be one but must complete two tasks first.'

'What tasks?'

Whatever they were, I was eager to help.

With my help, the tasks were simple.

First, Princess Apinya had to produce a talking cat.

Easy peasy, lemon squeezy.

The second was to get rid of Prince Nimcon Poop.

We achieved this easily with spell 85c, initially cast in Salem, Massachusetts in 1693 when a young maiden gave her suitor a repulse of her.

After Princess Apinya uttered a few words of what sounded like gibberish to the untrained ear and threw moonbeams into her suitor's drink, the horrified prince saw how his bride would look thirty years hence and promptly ended the engagement to marry another young miss.

Here's how we did it...

On my nocturnal wanderings, I caught a few moonbeams in a paw, stored them in my mouth, and Princess Apinya popped them in a jar. During the pre-wedding celebrations, she deftly emptied them into Prince Nimcon Poop's rice wine, and after one sip, he stared at her, screamed and ran away, saying, 'I will not marry a hideous hag.'

The next day a young, handsome prince appeared, far more prosperous than Prince Nimcon Poop, and asked the king for his daughter's hand in marriage.

BAKING AND ENTERING

Relieved, the king said, 'You can have more than her hand, my boy. Take her entire body with my blessing.'

The Princess, spying with me at an open doorway, gave an unroyal whoop and said, 'He's going to take my entire body, Prija. I can't wait because he's gorgeous.'

'Show some decorum,' I hissed, inwardly thrilled.

It turned out the prince was a warlock, Princess Apinya became his witch princess, and I became their familiar, and we did much magic and much good together.

Sadly, universal magic did not bless them with eternal life, and I was passed on to their eldest daughter. And so on.

In 1880 my current princess and I travelled to Baden, Germany, on a magic carpet. There, we met Queen Victoria, who, naturally, fell in love with me.

'We must import these beautiful cats into England,' she said.

From then, I adored the idea of England, as did my current witch princess. She moved to Surrey with me and married a warlock duke in 1883 when we all moved into Gropely Hall in Kent.

Everywhere I went, people exclaimed at my beauty, and Mr Owen Gould, who came for tea one day, was so enraptured by me he imported a breeding pair of Siamese cats, Pho and Mia. Of course, they were less remarkable than I and not magic.

Pho and Mia had a litter of kittens that appeared at the Crystal Palace Cat Show in 1885.

If it weren't for my ability to turn invisible at the flick of my elegant tail, some evil person would likely have stolen me due to the understandable clamour for the glamour of Siamese cats.

Humans and witches like to think they own cats, but it's the reverse. I possessed many princess witches and prince warlocks until

I fell for a filthy-rich commoner in 1943. Sorry, I can't say his name as it's top-secret, but he helped end World War Two.

When he died, I was inconsolable, and the trauma diminished my magic, which allowed a vampire to steal me.

By the way, so as not to terrify Milly, I told her there is no such thing as blood-sucking vampires. Of course, that's untrue, but one fang at a time.

Anyhoo, this vampire threatened humankind (and catkind), and it took all my energy to oust him. At my lowest ebb, Prill appeared and rescued me.

All this, I told Milly, missing out a few points. One should not be too transparent – us cats must preserve our mystical auras. Oh, and I may have exaggerated a tad, but who wants a boring story?

Dream Treats

I couldn't assimilate Saphira's far-fetched tale. A magic carpet. Really? Although enough crazy stuff had happened to me recently so I shouldn't have been surprised.

Saphira rubbed her eyes. 'I hate to admit weakness but can't focus on the distant past anymore, as I'm a tad twitchy, awaiting the results of that karma spell.'

Worried, I said, 'When will we know?'

'Anytime now.'

'What was the spell exactly?'

'You heard Prill say it?'

'Yes, but what should happen?'

'Get me a few Dream Treats, then I'll tell you.'

I smiled. Dream Treats were the only cat food Saphira would eat. Colin would sell his soul (or mine) for them.

'Get them yourself,' I said contrarily.

'No – they are in the top cupboard in the kitchen, and I don't have the energy to leap.'

'Salmon, tuna or chicken?'

'Chocolate.'

'Don't be silly – there is no chocolate flavour.'

After a cheeky wink, she said, 'Yes, there is – I just created them.'

'If you can create them, why can't you spirit them here?'

'You humans want magic explained in a neat little package. You can't explain magic. Can you explain intuition?'

'Sort of – it's a hunch.'

'Can you explain good luck?'

'That's self-explanatory,' I said.

'Yes – but is it random?'

'I guess so. What are you saying?'

'That magic is random. Some days witches, warlocks, and familiars are capable of certain feats, and other days it takes every ounce of energy to cast the most basic spells. Like cars, our tanks can't run on empty, and we need Dream Treats, or whatever.'

'Message received and understood.' Reluctantly, I rose from my cosy slumped position and headed to the kitchen, muttering, 'Chocolate Dream Treats, indeed.'

On tiptoe, I opened the top cupboard, and at the front was an unopened packet of Chocolate Dream Treats for Pampered Cats.

Saphira held out an eager paw. 'Quick, I'm dying of hunger here.'

About to say, 'Don't be dramatic,' I realised I was desperate for peanut butter on toast.

I left Saphira munching Dream Treats and headed for the kitchen again. As I did, there was an almighty bang on the door and a frenzied shout. 'Let me in. Something awful has happened.'

Trepidatious, I opened the door, and Sebastian fell into my arms sobbing, 'Damien is dead.'

It took two mugs of tea laced with whisky and two rounds of peanut butter and strawberry jam on toast to calm him down. Of course, I joined him in the feast, claiming shock, despite not being surprised.

Sebastian said Damien was dead, killed in a car crash on the A3 out of London. 'There were two women in the car with Damien, and they're also dead,' he sobbed.

I fell into a trap when I said, 'How did you find out so quickly?'

Despite his apparent grief, Sebastian's eyes narrowed. 'What do you mean, so quickly? I didn't say when it happened.'

I was saved by the bell when Prill swept into the room, unseen and unheard by Sebastian, and said to me, 'Say you meant how come the police informed him when he's not next of kin.'

So, I looked Sebastian square in his lovely face and said, 'I mean, how come the police told you when you're not next of kin?'

He flushed a pretty shade of peach. 'My sister is in the police. Hers was the first car at the scene. She couldn't wait to tell me Damien was dead as she didn't trust him from the outset. Mummy hated him too, called him a mean-featured ferret.'

'Why didn't your sister stay with you this evening?' I said.

'Had to get back to work – and she'd double-parked the Ford Granada.'

It seemed a cruel way to break bad news. Not wishing to be insensitive myself, I said, 'Why was she in such a rush to tell you?'

'Because Mummy said if I didn't renounce Damien by midnight tonight, she would cut me off.'

Why do so many rich kids call their mothers Mummy after the age of ten? I knew no working-class kid who did. My theory is it's a suck-up tactic connected with all that dosh. 'Surely your mum would have relented anyway once Damien was dead,' I said.

'You don't know her. It had to be of my own volition.'

'What if she discovers you heard the news before you renounced Damien?'

'She won't – trust me. Sis has it covered.'

After a glance at my watch, I said, 'You'd best call your mum if millions are at stake.'

'Already did.'

'But you were utterly devastated when you came to my door.'

His face creased in a cheeky grin. 'Ah, my acting fooled you?'

'Acting?'

'Yes. I'm relieved, not devastated – as if an evil spell has broken. Damien held me in some vile grip. He wasn't even handsome and had a spotty bum.'

He rose from the sofa and danced around the room, wiggling his delicious hips provocatively. As he did, he spotted Saphira and said, 'Hello, darling cat, haven't seen you in ages.'

When Sebastian left, I fondly surveyed Prill and Saphira, curled up together and said, 'Please fill in the missing pieces.'

Prill raised her eyebrows. 'All that matters is the terrible trio is dead, and I hope that's the last we hear of them.'

'Were they magical?'

'Damien was a demonic dark warlock, and Stella and her mother under his spell.'

I shuddered. 'What if Damien returns from the dead?'

'It's unlikely, and if so, not for some time. Let's not put more attention on evil than necessary – leave well alone.'

But I needed to know one more thing. 'So are the two dead women definitely Stella and her mother?'

'Yes. Justice has been done,' said Prill. 'Stella caused Holly's death in a car, the other two were equally evil, and natural law reacted accordingly. Simple. Magic can only hurry karma along a little.'

'Meaning?'

'We don't know if my spell or fate caused the crash.'

Hmm – odd that Sebastian's sister was a policewoman and first at the scene. So many unanswered questions and general weirdness.

Prill waved a hand and said, 'Hot off the press, tell of the deaths.'

In a puff of blue smoke, a pink-paged newspaper appeared on the coffee table.

'Check the headline, Milly,' said Prill.

The newspaper's name, *Ahead of the Times*, made me giggle as I scanned the front page.

The headline was…

Three Died Instantly When a Car Crashed Into a Barrier on the A3.

The article said no other cars were involved, although a witness saw a Siamese cat run from the wreckage.

I showed Saphira the article.

'Not I,' she said casually. 'But I can confirm the deceased are the terrible trio.'

Prill clapped a hand to her mouth.

'What's the matter?' I said.

'Robbie is free from that awful woman and is probably unconnected with my demise. Holly heard pillow talk as Stella plotted but didn't mention Robbie's replies. Perhaps he was asleep at the time.'

I'd be the same with my daughter, willing to grasp any straw of hope, however flimsy.

'Why not ask him?' I said.

'Darling, I'm dead. But you could.'

'How?'

'As you know, he usually frequents Banters Brasserie on Saturday mornings. I saw the passionate glance you both exchanged last time.'

'But he won't go this week if he's grieving.'

'And if he's not grieving, he may go to celebrate.'

'But he might not go alone.' The thought of Robbie with another woman made my tummy clench with jealousy.

My mind and hormones were in a whirl. If Robbie were innocent, I must return my inheritance, but maybe we'd have a chance at love (or lust). If he weren't, Prill would be devastated, but I'd keep my inheritance. But how to explain it all?

With a shudder, I envisaged myself back in Fairley with minimal funds.

'Or, I'll find out right now,' said Prill.

'How?'

'On the top shelf of your fitted wardrobe is a crystal ball wrapped in red silk. Be a darling and fetch it.'

'It wasn't there earlier.'

'Please check.'

I did – and of course, it was there.

'Will you look into the future?' I asked Prill.

'No, darling – the past – to the night Holly heard pillow talk. I will survey what happened in that bedroom.'

'Why didn't you do that before?'

Prill raised a mocking brow. 'This crystal ball is akin to a technicolour screen, so, as a mother, you know the answer.'

Guiltily, I nodded – I wouldn't want to see nasty truths about my child enacted before my eyes. Knowing is one level of torture; seeing it, worse. Now, almost sure of Robbie's innocence, Prill was willing to risk what she previously had not.

Saphira flicked her tail – a sign of feline anxiety Colin often employed.

Although I had no tail to flick, I hadn't been this nervous since my second driving test in 1965.

Brow furrowed, Prill peered into the globe and muttered something unintelligible.

After what seemed hours, but according to my Timex, was ten minutes, she clutched her throat and said, 'My son is innocent. I surveyed the bedroom incident Holly described, and Robbie was fast asleep as Stella plotted my demise. Then I viewed him during my funeral, and he was genuinely distraught. He's my son, so I know the signs.'

Saphira leapt the two yards from her sofa to Prill's knee in a rare show of obvious enthusiasm and said, 'Such good news.'

Selfishly, my first thought was of myself. Perhaps Robbie would fall in love with me. But what would a gorgeous hunk want with Milly Miller? Because despite Sebastian's assurances, I was no supermodel, and my wrinkles and greying hair didn't help. Stella had been scary looking but still model material – for the London Dungeon at Madame Tussauds.

That was catty (sorry, Saphira) – Stella's features had been perfect, albeit fierce. But I doubted they were after the crash. But perhaps she wore a seatbelt and avoided windscreen laceration of her perfectly proportioned visage.

To get the inevitable over with, I said, 'I must return my inheritance, Prill.'

She shook her head. 'Don't be hasty. There is much to ponder and discover before such big decisions.'

'Such as what? Have you kept things from me?'

'Full marks for genius,' scoffed Saphira. 'There is much we've kept from you. If we told you everything at once, you'd go crazy as your consciousness isn't expanded enough. After two centuries, even I am often shocked by magic and coincidences.'

'Are they always two separate things?' I said.

'It's often impossible to separate the two. But with a good result, what does the cause matter? Humans are obsessed with analysis.'

In defence of humans, I said, 'If something works, analysis helps recreate it.'

'Only tangible and mechanical stuff, but magical and esoteric phenomena are usually impossible to quantify, analyse or repeat, but you humans insist on trying.'

A tad miffed at Saphira's arrogant tone, I said, 'Give me an example, Miss Clever Claws.'

Emulating Rodin's The Thinker sculpture, she rested her chin on the back of a paw then said, 'Enlightenment.'

'A big subject. What do you mean?'

Prill joined in. 'If someone becomes enlightened whilst washing dishes, it doesn't mean that washing dishes caused enlightenment, merely that the accumulation of experience happened whilst someone washed dishes, but it could have happened any time, unconnected with the activity. However, people who hear the tale will wash dishes and expect instant enlightenment.'

I laughed. 'But it would be a good ruse.'

'Yes, I should have used it on Bill. He was a good husband but hated washing up.'

Expression serious, tone ominous, she said, 'Milly?'

'Yes?'

I expected terrible tidings, but she simply said, 'I can't use the crystal ball anymore.'

'Never?'

'Temporarily. It uses a lot of magical energy, and I need to refuel. I must investigate Robbie further before I make some difficult decisions.'

'And?' The hairs at the nape of my neck prickled.

'Please go to Banters Brasserie on Saturday?'

'Why?'

'I want him to invite you to his table. Or vice versa.'

'How do you know he'll be there?'

'I don't.'

Saphira piped up, 'I have enough magic left to ensure he turns up at 10 am. You should arrive at 10.15, Milly.'

I surveyed them both. 'And then what?'

'Leave it to the universe,' said Prill with a wink. 'And a drop of my special vanilla.'

'For him or me?'

'Him. Pop a drop in his tea or coffee, and it will bring out his true uninhibited self.'

Oh, my stars. I tried to appear calm as X-rated lustful fantasies played in my mind.

A Shopping Spree

The next day I awoke optimistic and excited. Was it the inheritance? No – because I might lose it to Robbie. Was it Robbie? No, because I wasn't a teenager and knew an ongoing romantic relationship was (sadly) pure fantasy. Still, a girl could dream.

What then?

I searched my brain until it hit me...

I was myself for the first time since Mike died.

Hopefully, I would see Robbie on Saturday, but my happiness did not depend on the outcome.

Or so I told myself.

After I hopped from bed, I surveyed the wardrobe for something suitable (sexy) to wear on Saturday.

Apart from the tracksuit, my drab clothes suited a Puritan church gathering. When did I lose my fashion mojo? No wonder Prill didn't take me on buying trips after that first foray to London. When I married Steve, I'd unconsciously preserved my personality and fashion sense in aspic.

No wonder life had been dull and robotic.

A whoosh of joy shot through me. Perhaps it wasn't too late. Flinging off my pyjamas, I surveyed myself in the mirrored wardrobe door. My hair was an unruly mop, I had lines around my eyes, and my mouth turned down slightly at the corners. But apart from a few stretch marks and wobbly bits, my body wasn't bad for its age.

When Mum visited last Christmas, she said, 'You dress like your paternal grandma, but you used to be snazzy. What happened?'

When my eyes filled with tears, she apologised and changed the subject.

As we ate Christmas cake and supped tea, the answer to my granny-style hit me – I didn't want to encourage passion with Steve.

And if my clothes were boring, my asexual pyjamas and high-necked nighties belonged in a convent.

Things had to change. Even if I returned the inheritance, I had enough money for a fashion splurge.

After a quick shower, I threw on brown trousers, a beige blouse, shoved my feet into style-free sandals, gathered my brown handbag, dashed downstairs, and knocked on Fawn's door. *Please let her be off work today or at least on a late shift.*

She wasn't due in work until 5 pm.

'Come shopping, and I'll treat you to lunch,' I said.

'Give me ten minutes to dress.'

We caught the tube from South Kensington to Oxford Street. After we exited the dark underground into bright sunshine, we nipped to a cafe for coffees and pastries and were lucky to nab a sunny pavement table.

As Fawn chatted about her hectic social life, I felt a pang and wished my daughter didn't live so far north. But now free, I could see her more. But what if the inheritance were no longer mine? I'd have to get another humdrum job to make ends meet.

Fawn raised an eyebrow. 'You look like you lost a pound and found ten pence.'

'Strange, as I awoke in a fabulous mood.'

'No day is all bad or all good,' she said with wisdom beyond her years.

About to reply, my dad's funeral day was grim throughout, I realised it was untrue. My favourite uncle made me laugh so much about Dad's childhood antics I nearly choked. In bed that night, although heartbroken, I counted my blessings that such a cheerful, kind man had been my dad. I'd always have the memories and thought of him every day.

As I wiped away a tear, Fawn said, 'Here's our order now, thank God – I'm starving and need a caffeine shot.'

After a foamy sip of cappuccino, Fawn wiped her mouth. 'What's the plan, Stan?'

'I want to reinvent myself.'

Fawn pursed her lips in contemplation. 'Start with the onelength hair as it does you no favours – you need face-framing layers. Then we'll hit the makeup department in Havens department store on Bond Street where I worked when I first moved to London. Then the Way Out boutique on the top floor.'

'Aren't I too old for a boutique?'

'Nope. Mum bought a few outfits there recently, and she's more ancient than you.'

'You cheeky young whippersnapper.'

Fawn smiled as she perused the menu.

'Are you still hungry?' I said.

'No – but you can snack all day here.'

'How do you mean?'

'In Blossoms between noon and 3 pm, we only admit those who want a full lunch. Loads of places in London are like that. If you fancy coffee and croissant or tea and scones for lunch in a stylish cafe, it's nigh impossible. If I had my way, I'd put a lots of small tables in Blossoms and let people order what they want all day, every day.'

While a flamboyant man cut my hair in Top Knots salon, Fawn visited her old friends in Havens.

When we met up outside Marks and Spencer, she said, 'Wow! That cut takes years off you.'

I patted my hair, now at chin rather than shoulder level. 'Thanks – I'm pleased with it.'

In Havens, Fawn took me to the Elspeth Arden counter, where her friend gave me a makeover. After she applied what felt like thick layers of foundation and powder, masses of eyeshadow and oodles of mascara, I expected to resemble a pantomime dame.

'The magenta lipstick and fuchsia blush are perfect for your cool colouring, and the marine shadow makes your blue eyes pop. Ready for the grand unveiling? said the consultant.

I'd refused a mirror (and an anaesthetic) and was reluctant to view my face, despite Fawn's enthusiasm from the sideline. Used to my almost-not-there makeup, I imagined I'd resemble 'mutton dressed as lamb'. The latter was a cardinal sin, according to my ex-mother-in-law.

'Okay,' I said.

Fawn produced a hand mirror, which she held in front of me as I closed my eyes. 'Open your eyes, cowardly custard,' she said.

I did. Was that me? Oh, my God. I would resemble my younger, prettier sister if I had one. My eyes were brighter, my lips lusher, my cheekbones higher, yet it looked natural.

'We'll buy everything you used,' said Fawn to her friend.

Unsure of my present and future bank balance, I began, 'But...'

'No buts – my treat – my boyfriend's family owns this store, and I get a massive discount.'

'Which boyfriend?' I said.

'Tarquin. He's flying me to his family's Scottish castle in a helicopter tomorrow.'

'Wow – how exciting. Have you been on one before?'

'No. I'm worried the blades will chop my head off.'

I thought of JR from Dallas ducking as he got on and off the Ewing Oil helicopter. 'Keep your head down, and you'll be fine. Anyway, the blades are higher than they look.'

'Let's hope.'

After the assistant handed me a yellow carrier bag, I said to Fawn, 'What next?'

'The boutique.'

'Great – but I insist on paying.'

'Fine – but use my discount.'

Never one to presume, I said, 'Are you sure?'

'Yes. I can tell you're no user. I don't tell certain unscrupulous acquaintances about my discount.'

'How do you know I'm not unscrupulous?'

'I'm blessed with brilliant intuition.'

That's what Prill had said.

Cast not a clout until May is out is a truism. The balmy weather had turned cold, and Michael Fish had forecast rain for the weekend.

I chose a hot-pink wool skirt suit, hemline two inches above the knee, and a grey silk blouse for my restaurant rendezvous. Fawn bought a clingy red dress with enormous shoulder pads and diamante studs, its hemline ten inches above the knee, for Saturday night in the castle.

'Are you sure you won't be cold?' I said, sounding mumsy. 'Perhaps wear a thermal vest underneath or buy something warmer.'

'I won't have it for long,' said Fawn with a saucy wink.

Blondes and Brollies

Saturday's dreary weather forecast was correct. Unwilling to spoil my snazzy new suit with a raincoat, I carried a bright pink brolly decorated with grey poodles. When I neared Banters Brasserie, I wished Prill were here, despite the awkwardness of the last visit. But a wall of bitter disappointment hit me when I spotted Robbie at a window table with a gorgeous blonde.

'Table for one, madam?' said the maître d'.

'Er yes, please. In a quiet corner – perhaps behind that pillar.' I pointed to a far table near the ladies' loo.

'Are you sure? How about that nice table in the window?' He gestured to a table next to Robbie and his blonde bombshell. 'Passers-by will love to see a lovely lady like yourself in the window.'

Huh. As if anyone would notice me next to Marilyn Monroe. How had I thought I had a chance with Robbie?

'Over there is fine, please.'

'Perhaps you should collapse your umbrella – a spoke could take someone's eye out.'

Inexplicably, I needed the umbrella to shield my face from Robbie. 'Er, I'll hold it high and collapse it when I reach my table.'

'As you wish, madam,' he said dubiously.

Telescopic umbrella in my handbag, I surveyed the menu through tears of bitter disappointment. I hadn't even met Robbie but felt jilted, thrown away like an old dish mop. What had been the point of the makeover? I would return north, buy a little property with the money from half the marital abode, and sell the promised pearls, although I doubted the latter would fetch much. Now Robbie appeared innocent, I should return the inheritance.

Marilyn Monroe sashayed past my table towards the loo. Perhaps to add more glossy coral lipstick to the perfect full mouth and brush the mane of shampoo-advert hair.

Imagining her in bed with Robbie, jealous bile filled my throat. I should sit next to them to eavesdrop on Prill's behalf, but I wasn't a masochist.

I kept my head down until Marilyn left the loo and passed me on a cloud of jasmine fragrance laced with sin. But instead of turning right towards Robbie, she turned left and sashayed towards a different table. At her wiggle-bummed approach, a divine dark-haired young man rose, kissed her, held out her chair, then they sat snuggled as they held hands atop the table.

Then – gasp – he went down on one knee, produced a small black velvet box, and opened it with a flourish as Marilyn screamed, 'Yes, yes, yes,' as if in the throes of sexual ecstasy.

Never happier to see two people engaged, I cheered and clapped along with the entire restaurant.

I caught Robbie's eye, and he smiled. I smiled back self-consciously, but he rose, crossed to my table and said, 'Don't hide such beauty in a corner. Join me at my table?'

'I'd be delighted, but who is the blonde?'

'A work acquaintance.'

After I ordered tea (my churning tummy didn't want food), we chatted.

'Did I see you here last Saturday?' he said.

Feigning nonchalance, I replied, 'Did you?'

'You were talking into a Dictaphone. Are you a writer?'

I thought fast. 'No. I'm selling my house after a divorce and remembered something to tell the solicitor.'

Wasn't I cunning to mention my divorce so soon?

Out of the blue, he said, 'My wife just died.'

Heart racing, I said, 'How awful, I'm so sorry.'

'Don't be. Stella was a nightmare, had me under a strange spell. I'm so relieved she's gone I won't even attend her funeral.'

It seemed strange he'd reveal this to a stranger, and I hadn't even used the magic vanilla. Buoyed by his company, I said, 'Why tell me – a stranger?'

'It's like I've known you all my life.' He frowned. 'Were you at a party in Liverpool's Adolpho hotel in the late 1960s?'

'Yes. I was the birthday girl.'

'I fell in love with you that evening, but Mum said to keep away as you'd just married.' His hand touched my arm as bolts of sexy electricity shot through me. 'After that, life, and Mum, got in the way and I never saw you again. Until recently.'

It was a romantic film.

Over drinks, we caught up on the last nearly twenty years.

Robbie had loved Holly and was devastated about her death and the time running up to it. 'It was weird. My wife and I loved each other. But I met Stella at the Duchess of Windsor's auction, and that was that.'

A blatant lie as the timing was wrong. 'That was in April this year and was all over the newspapers.'

The late Duchess of Windsor's jewellery sold for thirty-one million pounds, six times the expected amount, and some items fetched more than ten times the estimated price. Wow. I doubted all my jewellery would fetch as much as two hundred quid.

In ludicrous contrast, Elizabeth Taylor paid over four hundred thousand pounds for a plume-shaped diamond brooch designed in 1935 by the former Prince of Wales for his future bride. Ms Taylor was a close friend of the Duke and Duchess of Windsor, had often admired the brooch and after she acquired it, said, 'I loved it so much, I had to buy it. It's the first important jewel I've ever bought myself.'

Pulling me from my gems reverie, Robbie said, 'That was the jewellery auction in Switzerland. The Duchess of Windsor held a few private furniture auctions in Paris before her death. Anyway, I experienced a magnetic pull towards her.'

'Wallis?' I teased.

'Ha-ha. Funnily enough, she and Stella were peas in a pod.'

'You mean they looked alike?'

'Only their skinniness was similar – I mean a strange force they shared. I reckon the former Mrs Simpson had a negative, almost magical hold over Edward.'

'Perhaps Stella and Mrs Simpson were cut from the same coven.'

Robbie smiled. 'There's another reason I didn't pursue you.'

'Yes?'

'My ex gambling habit. I'm supposed to hear Mum's will soon, but deserve nothing.'

'Why?'

'I took enough of her money when she was alive.'

Tricky. I couldn't say I'd inherited the London flat and a pile of dosh. How to ask more questions without sounding mercenary?

I dived in the deep end. 'Was your mum very wealthy?'

'I'm not sure. There's maybe a house in Piddleton-on-Sea and a few thousand pounds. Although I suspect Mum sold the house to pay off debts and was embarrassed to tell me.'

'Why do you think she sold the house?'

'In her latter days she was always in London shacking up in a friend's flat and whenever I asked to visit, she changed the subject, saying it wasn't up to her usual standard. Oh, I could visit Piddleton-on-Sea for a recce but don't want to face unpalatable truths.'

'Unpalatable how?'

'I can't bear to think of mum as human as she always seemed magical, invincible. The idea of her in reduced circumstances is horrendous.'

Thinking of my current salubrious lodgings, it was almost funny, but time to change the subject.

Edging closer to his musky maleness, I said, 'So you fell in love with me all those years ago?'

'At first sight, and I'm in danger of falling for you all over again. It may have already happened.'

He stroked my face and looked deep into my eyes as my heart melted with happiness.

After two hours of bliss, Robbie had to leave, so we arranged a dinner date for Tuesday. 'Shall I pick you up from home?' he said.

Difficulties and possible farcical situations swam through my love-struck mind, so I said, 'Tuesday afternoon is frantic and unpredictable, so I'll meet you at the restaurant.'

'Okay, then – Capriccio, at eight – it's behind the Glitz Hotel.'

'I'll be there.'

BAKING AND ENTERING

He kissed my cheek then dashed away.

At home, Prill awaited me in the living room, face bright with anticipation. 'What happened?' she said.

'It was bliss, and I'm in love.'

As I told the story, Prill's smile widened, and she clasped her hands as if to say, 'I've dreamed of this day.'

'Did you know it would happen?'

'What, darling?' she said with an air of innocence.

'Robbie and I would get together. How did you know?'

'I didn't, but Bill did and told me recently.'

Was Prill's husband the missing link?

'Tell me about Bill,' I said.

Saphira, coiled on Prill's lap, said, 'I'm going out, as I can't take too much human amazement. The spiritually unevolved bore me.'

'And rude cats bore me,' I shot back.

'Tell that to a cat who cares.' Saphira padded across the carpet towards the door.

'What's eating her?' I asked Prill.

'It's what she's not eaten. Dolly served an inferior cut of smoked salmon earlier, and Saphira refused to eat it.'

Gosh – Saphira was contrary, but, again, nothing made sense. If Saphira conjured up Chocolate Dream Treats, why couldn't she conjure up the perfect smoked salmon?

I said as much to Prill, who replied, 'Darling, in the world of magic, don't expect logic or consistency.'

'How did Dolly know to buy salmon for Saphira?'

'Because Saphira wrote a note in your handwriting.'

'How did she hold the pen?'

'In her mouth. Darling, don't focus on minutiae. I have important things to discuss before you meet my son again. Capriccio, you say?'

'Yes.'

She wiped away a tear. 'It's the most romantic restaurant in the world, so Robbie must have romantic intentions. Tell me more; I'll try to fill in the gaps, then we'll plan.'

When I told Prill everything we'd discussed in Banters Brasserie, barring a few intimate details and sweet nothings, she said, 'My husband is a warlock...'

Prill and Bill

I didn't discover Bill was a warlock until I met Saphira. Bill hadn't met her before but envisaged her in a dream. From the age of ten, my husband knew he was a warlock. And he sensed I was to be his wife (and a witch) before we met. But although I had magical qualities, I would not know I was a witch for many years.

When Bill saw how happy I was living in Liverpool (in a gorgeous house opposite Sefton Park) and working in Togs, he temporarily shelved our agreement to move to Sussex.

My husband inherited magic from his mother. Much to his chagrin, Walter, Bill's identical twin, had no magic but this did not dim his love for my husband.

Walter was the 'Crown' in Crown and Scimitar Solicitors. He and Bill studied law at Oxford. I didn't take my husband's name, Crown, but kept my maiden name, Hodgkin.

When Bill, a higher warlock, died, he entered another realm, became Godlike, and asked Walter if he could help out occasionally. Mr Scimitar was long dead.

Thrilled and unperturbed by his dead brother's request, Walter said, 'By Jove, yes. I always wanted you in the business. We'll be like *Randall and Hopkirk (Deceased)*, except solicitors instead of detectives. What larks we'll have. You can deal with the, er, trickier cases.'

My death made it easier to be with Bill; both of us were now ethereal and could spirit ourselves anywhere. Once we sorted the slight mess with the will, we would holiday in France and Italy with a spell to make us look and act alive for a few weeks, able to eat and drink.

'Oh, think of the food and wines,' I said to Saphira.

I told this story to Milly in the relaxing soporific tone I once used for Robbie's bedtime stories. That way, I thought the revelation about Bill and me would be less scary.

I was right.

After I mentioned *Randall and Hopkirk*, her eyelids fluttered and she said, 'What an amazing story, Prill. Do you mind if I go to bed?'

'No, darling – sweet dreams.'

Minutes after Milly headed to bed, Bill materialised in a bespoke midnight-blue evening suit and pink bow tie.

When Milly said she saw him in a starry cloak, I knew it was a dream, not a vision, as Bill would not stoop to such showy vulgarity. 'Save it for the circus,' he would say.

'Darling, he said. Where shall we go tonight?'

'Paris?'

'Hold my hand, and I'll take you there.'

After ten minutes of floating through a sultry night sky, we were on the banks of the moonlit Seine.

'What shall we do about the will?' said Bill.

'Perhaps wait a while, see if Milly and Robbie get together?'

'Fate will not stand in their way as it did in the past. But here's what to do.' He whispered in my ear.

'Oh, that's genius, Bill, and leaves them with free will.'

Easy Come, Easy Go

Minutes after I woke on Monday, Prill appeared at my bedside. 'Get dressed, Milly. Mr Crown wants to see you in his office – a limousine will collect you in fifteen minutes.'

'Am I to return the inheritance?' I said.

'Wait and see.'

Crown and Scimitar had a new assistant, one a lot friendlier than Stella's mum – not difficult.

'Mr Crown will see you now,' she beamed.

When I entered the office, I was unsure if Mr Crown was Bill or Walter, but it seemed impolite to ask. But when he turned a tad phosphorescent, I knew it was Bill.

He handed me a document and said, 'This is the amended will. Priscilla Hodgkin did not bequeath you a London flat and a hundred thousand pounds.'

That was that. My short-lived career as an heiress was over.

'Why so crestfallen, dear?' said Bill.

'I'm not – easy come, easy go,' I lied.

'Oh, my dear, nothing in your favour has changed. But it was not Priscilla Hodgkin who bequeathed you the flat and money but Audrey Bleasdale.'

'Audrey Bleasdale?' The name rang a distant bell.

'Er – yes. I think so. But what about the other residents of 28 Queen Avenue?'

'Whatever you told them or intimated, they will recall Prill renting the flat from her friend and Audrey bequeathing it to you. If asked, do not offer more information. Least said, soonest mended in all walks of life. Don't hang dirty washing on the line for all to see.'

'No, of course. And Piddleton-on-Sea?'

'What about it?'

'Who is that bequeathed to?'

'That, my dear, is none of your business. And if it becomes your business because of some, er, romantic entanglement, then time will tell. Will that be all?'

'Yes. Thanks.'

I hesitated at the door. 'So, I still own 28c Queen Avenue and the money?'

'Yes. All is as before apart from me fixing a slight error.'

Spooning in June

I saw Robbie a few times a week. Although our mutual attraction was unmistakable, enamoured with our new relationship, it was unspoken we didn't wish to rush something so precious.

Our romance was still platonic – apart from the most amazing prolonged kisses, which made my heart fizz and toes curl. We were at the beginning of a long love banquet we didn't wish to rush. We wanted to savour every juicy bite as we exquisitely teased ourselves as we awaited dessert.

The fast food could wait a while.

In between heavenly time with Robbie, I hung out with Fawn, Sebastian or Peter – sometimes all three at once. Dolly was a regular visitor, kept 28c spick and span and gave me many a laugh.

On one of Prill's starry-eyed visits away from Bill, I asked her why the will stipulated that I employ Dolly for a few years.

'No mystery there – she's a treasure I didn't want you to lose. Was I right?'

I thought of Dolly's colourful, cheerful presence, and amazing cleaning powers and simply said, 'Yes.'

Saphira was her usual amusing arrogant self, happy as long as her smoked salmon and prawn supply met her high feline standards.

BAKING AND ENTERING

On a Tuesday, about 3 pm, Robbie phoned and suggested we meet by the Serpentine.

We often strolled around Hyde Park, stopped to buy vanilla ice-cream cones, then enjoyed them on a bench by the Serpentine Lake. It was a balmy June and too lovely to be indoors.

Robbie met me, eyes shining, and said, 'I heard Mum's Last Will and Testament earlier.'

'And?'

'She left me the Piddleton-on-Sea house, the business premises and a pearl necklace.'

I couldn't remember what I should know, so said in an innocent voice, 'Business premises?'

'Yes. Mum had a cafe called Baking and Entering, which I will turn into an antique shop.'

'Why an antique shop?'

'That's how I make money since I gave up gambling. It suits my personality as I buy on intuition, so it's a gamble I'll profit. Didn't I mention my business?'

'No.' He'd mentioned the furniture auction, but I didn't make a connection.

Without preamble, he said, 'Marry me and live in Piddleton-on-Sea?'

Dizzy with happy shock, something stopped me saying *yes*. Much as I loved Robbie, I also loved myself – at long last. I took his hand, looked into his eyes and said, 'I love you but don't want to remarry. Not yet, anyway. And it might spoil what we have. Let's just enjoy being us for a while.'

Had I upset him? He took a while to respond, and I held my breath. Had I sabotaged something wonderful?

Eventually, he said, 'I only proposed as I don't want to lose you. Let's have an un-marriage, like Humpty Dumpty's un-birthdays. Un-marry me, Milly? And we'll visit each other often.'

I loved the idea of a dual life between London and Piddleton-on-Sea. 'It sounds perfect.'

'Shall we shop for unmarried rings tomorrow?' he said, eyes twinkling with love and fun.

Fun – the main missing ingredient of my marriage to Steve.

'That would be lovely.'

I drifted home on a cloud of romantic happiness and entered my flat, which seemed more mine than ever due to Prill often being away with Bill. Saphira, typical cat, was present when it suited her, where she was the rest of the time, was anyone's guess.

As I sat down with a cup of tea and a chocolate digestive biscuit, the phone rang. It was a tearful Fawn. 'Can I pop up for a chat?'

'Yes, do. The kettle has just boiled.'

Clutching a mug, Fawn said, 'I've lost my job as someone is taking over the cafe.'

'Tell me more.'

'My current boss is moving to Florida with his boyfriend, and the person who wants to take over hates me.'

'Why?'

'I won't go out with him.'

'Ah, I see – blackmail?'

'Yes – but I won't be bought. I asked the landlord about the rent, and it's steep. Tarquin will put up half the rent for a profit share, but I need to find my half.'

I doubted Tarquin had a Lady Diana Spencer waiting in the wings and was set on Fawn. 'Is it a viable concern?' I said.

'A goldmine.'

'Fancy me as a partner?'

'You're kidding?'

'No, I'm not. I can't think of anything more exciting than running a London cafe.'

Fawn whooped then yawned. 'Sorry, I had a bit too much to drink due to the upset. Can we continue this chat tomorrow?'

'Of course.'

'You won't change your mind?'

'Never in a million years.' It felt right.

When Fawn left, Saphira appeared and said, 'I listened in, and you did the right thing. Ah, here's Prill.'

'I suppose you heard everything, too?' I said.

'Yes, darling. It couldn't be more perfect; let me explain.'

'Please do.'

'You know about my magic vanilla recipe?'

'Yes.'

'It was the main reason Baking and Entering was successful. Plus, it did good in the community, increased Ojalis and all that.'

'And?'

'I hoped you'd continue Baking and Entering in Piddleton-on-Sea but fate intended otherwise. But perhaps you could continue it with Fawn.'

'In the London cafe?'

'Yes.'

'But I don't want to sell books. Not to begin with, anyway.' A cafe on King's Road would be busy enough without complicating matters, and I couldn't imagine learning two new businesses at once.

'What *do* you want?'

I thought for a while. 'There are few places in London where you can just have tea, coffee and/or a snack without a full meal. I'd like a Parisian-style Cafe with small round tables.'

'Does Fawn want the same?'

'I haven't asked, but I think so. When we had breakfast in a little cafe off Oxford Street, she said something similar.'

'I'll give you my magic vanilla recipe.'

'The one that increases Ojalis, brings out people's good points and makes them happy?'

'Yes.'

'I think not.'

Prill looked crestfallen, and I couldn't let her suffer. 'Only joking, it sounds brilliant. But as I'm not a witch, will the recipe work?'

'Saphira will help. What will you call the premises?'

'If Fawn agrees, Scone but Not Forgotten, in memory of you.'

'I'll visit often, darling.'

'I know, but the name is fun.'

'Yes, it is.'

'I like it,' said Saphira.

Praise indeed.

Epilogue

The Fairley house was officially sold, and the new owners, a young couple with a baby girl, would move in on the 12th of July. As Steve was still in America, I nipped north to sort things out. At least I thought Steve was still in America but hadn't spoken to him for a week as we kept missing each other and whenever I phoned one hotel, he'd already moved to the next leaving just a message. I imagined he was avoiding me, but why?

As I entered my old home, a wave of nostalgia swept over me. Was my former life so bad? Not really, but it had been dull, humdrum. Part of me wanted it back as my new magical life scared me as it was overwhelming to be surrounded by witches, warlocks and a talking cat. Well, one witch, one warlock and one talking cat, to be exact.

Mrs Snoops' nosiness antennae were in complete working order. As soon as I put the kettle on, the doorbell rang.

'Hello, Mrs Miller,' she said from the doorstep. 'Have you left London for good?'

'Just for a few days. And as I keep saying, please call me Milly.'

She sniffed with disapproval. 'No, it's not the done thing, Mrs Miller. May I have a word? It's important.'

I hid a sigh as I'd planned a long bath after the sticky train journey, but she seemed troubled, near to tears.

'Come in, Mrs Snoops. It will have to be black tea or coffee as I haven't shopped for milk. But I should be able to rustle up a packet of Hobnobs.'

'I'll fetch a jug of milk from next door. Back in a mo.'

When we settled on a chair apiece, I said, 'How's Colin?'

In a strangled voice, Mrs Snoops said, 'That's what I want to talk to you about.'

My blood chilled. Had Colin been run over, had he run away? 'Is he alright?' I said.

'Yes, but I'm not.'

As her demeanour resembled someone en route to the gallows, I imagined she was ill and hoped it wasn't terminal. I leaned forwards, put a reassuring hand on her arm and softly said, 'What's the matter?'

She sobbed out, 'I can't bear to lose him.'

Golly. Was her son ill? She idolised that man. I knew it wasn't her husband as he'd died three years earlier. 'Who can't you bear to lose, Mrs Snoops?'

She looked at me beseechingly. 'I can't bear to lose Colin, the light of my life.'

There was only one thing for it. 'Then he's yours, Mrs Snoops.'

Her face lit up like a five-year-old's at Christmas. 'Really?'

'Yes. Where is Colin now, by the way?'

'Curled up on my bed after a lovely plate of boned trout.'

If reincarnation were true, I vowed to return as a cat.

But I dreaded breaking the Colin news to my daughter.

There was no time like the present, so when a happy Mrs Snoops left, I nervously dialled a Northumberland number as my heart sped.

'Hello, Mum. Where are you? I just phoned London but got no answer. I have news I'm not sure you'll like.'

Heart racing, I didn't care what the news was as long as my daughter wasn't ill.

'Are you sitting down, Mum?'

That old chestnut – she was definitely ill. What was it? Cancer? A brain tumour? I must stop watching medical dramas. 'Spit it out before I have a heart attack.'

I held my breath as she said, 'John and I are splitting up, and I'm off to Australia with a girlfriend for a year.'

Golly – I wasn't expecting that. 'Australia?' I said faintly. 'Why?'

'For an adventure – we'll pick fruit, wash dishes or something, but the thing is, Mum, I can't take Colin.'

Disappointment at Kaye's far-flung location changed to relief, and I could breathe again. 'That's fine, love.'

'Will you take Colin to London, Mum, or will Dad have him? I can't get hold of Dad, by the way.'

'Actually, love...'

To my amazement, Kaye was happy with the Mrs Snoops arrangement. 'Oh, that's great, Mum. I knew the nosy cow had a soft spot for Colin. He's landed on his paws and won't have to leave his territory.'

One worry sorted, I phoned Cheryl's home, but a stranger answered and said, 'She moved out last week.'

'Did she leave a forwarding address?'

'Maybe.'

'Why maybe?'

'She said to only give it to one person. What's your name?'

'Milly Miller.'

'That's her. What's your favourite soup?'

This was crazy. 'Favourite soup? Why?'

'Dunno, but Cheryl said to only give the number to a woman called Milly Miller whose favourite soup is p – whoops, nearly gave the game away.'

Bemused, I said, 'My favourite soup is pea and ham.' After dinner at Capriccio, it was now lobster bisque, but Cheryl wouldn't know that.

'She's at the Flamenco hotel in Las Vegas for another week, room 202; after that, you'll find her at...'

I rang the Vegas hotel. 'Room 202, please.'

'Putting you through, ma'am.'

The phone rang about five times, and a breathless but familiar voice answered. It couldn't be. It was.

My ex-husband – Steve.

Confused, I said, 'I was given this number for Cheryl.'

'Yes, that's right. We got married yesterday. Would you like to speak to my wife?'

'Er, yes.'

Too weird.

'Hello, Milly,' said Cheryl. 'I hope you don't mind.'

'Er, no, not really. But, how, when, why?'

Cheryl's bold voice said, 'Steve, bugger off to the bar so I can talk to Milly in peace.'

Gosh, I'd never spoken to him like that; perhaps it was what he'd craved.

When I heard, 'Okay, you wonderful woman,' I knew I was right.

As direct and guileless as ever, Cheryl said, 'Steve lost your London number and phoned me at Feet First to see if I had it. One thing led to another, and he invited me to America.'

I had a million questions, couldn't form a sentence, and muttered, 'But...'

'Remember the Feet First Christmas party two years ago, Milly?'

'Yes, you and Steve got on like a house on fire.'

'We really hit it off, but I damped any romantic dreams as he was my mate's husband.'

I racked my brains to remember if Cheryl had encouraged me to end the marriage. No – not once, although she'd been pleased for me (and probably for herself) when I was finally free. But could I fault her as a friend?

No.

Then she said something that shot her even higher in my estimation. 'I'm holding you to that dinner at Oodles of Noodles. Just the two of us.'

Tears filled my eyes as I said. 'It's a done deal, and I have loads to tell you.'

My exciting new life awaited, and I couldn't be happier, despite the scary magical elements.

Want to continue reading Milly's Midlife Adventures?
Follow the link to read Scone but Not Forgotten[1]

---

1. https://books2read.com/sconebutnotforgotten

Scone but Not Forgotten Blurb

Can she save her daughter from a dastardly demon? Oh, and solve a murder in her spare time?

Newly divorced and forty, Milly's life takes a magical turn for the better. She has a fabulous London pad, a hunky boyfriend, and a hip new cafe on King's Road, Chelsea. She even counts royalty amongst her customers.

What could go wrong?

Everything.

Someone murders her landlord, and Milly turns amateur sleuth to avert a miscarriage of justice. Then customers disappear into a time-tunnel, lured by a vengeful, greedy demon. When he threatens Milly's daughter's life, the gloves are off.

With the help of a friendly witch ghost and a sassy 200-year-old talking cat, can Milly travel to Regency London and save her daughter?

If you enjoy zany paranormal comedies with plenty of magical mystery and a dash of romance, you'll love Scone but Not Forgotten...

Find out more [1]

---

1. https://books2read.com/sconebutnotforgotten

Scone but Not Forgotten Extract

New Beginnings

Tuesday, August 11th, 1987

A tall, slim young woman in a large-brimmed straw hat, jeans and a silk shirt said, 'When does it open?'

Fawn and I were outside our cafe admiring the new pink signwriting on a grey background – Scone but Not Forgotten.

'Next Monday,' I said proudly.

'Will there be an opening party?'

I was about to say no when Fawn said, 'Yes – this Saturday evening – the 15th. Give us your address, and we'll send the details.'

We hadn't planned a party, but it now seemed a great idea.

The woman laughed. 'You don't recognise me?'

'You remind me of Princess Diana,' I ventured nervously.

The lookalike gurgled with laughter. 'I am she, and I'll rustle up a few friends to attend.'

I wanted to ask if she would grace us with her presence but was unsure how to address her, but Fawn had no such scruples and said, 'Will you come too, Di?'

Golly – that was rather forward. I had visions of Fawn dragged to the Tower of London and unceremoniously beheaded until Princess Diana said, 'How delightful to be referred to in such a casual fashion. So refreshing. I have obligations that evening, but my distant cousin, Lady Elvira, might attend. Looks like me, but has long dark hair, brown eyes, and wears funkier clothes.'

From under the floppy hat brim, she winked a blue eye and strolled away.

Fawn snapped her fingers and said, 'I knew it.'

'Knew what?'

'Don't you read the gossip columns?'

'No.' Any spare time I had was spent with my nose in a romance or murder mystery. I was currently devouring a Marion Chesney Regency series – unusual, as I usually read contemporary stuff. But when I'd nipped into Waterstones to buy the latest Sue Grafton, I spotted the Regency display and couldn't resist the adorable covers depicting swooning heroines and dastardly dukes.

However, Fawn pulled me to the present when she said, 'Lady Elvira is the latest it-girl, sprung up from nowhere. Rumour has it she's Princess Diana in disguise.'

'Gosh – how exciting. Will we be ready for this Saturday?'

'We'd better be. We might have royalty attending.'

I wanted to pinch myself, as I couldn't believe how quickly my life had changed from drab to fab.

Earlier in 1987, I got divorced after twenty uneventful, dreary years. I'd worked in Feet First, a shoe shop in Liverpool, and life plodded along.

The day the decree-absolute arrived, I also inherited a London flat and a wad of money from Prill, a recently deceased old boss. When her ghost visited me, we discovered she hadn't lost her magical powers. Unbeknownst to me, she'd been a witch when alive.

With Fawn's help, along with the assistance of a 200-year-old talking cat (the bane of my life, much as I love her), I solved Prill's murder. And I inherited a gorgeous boyfriend, Prill's son, who had an antique shop in Piddleton-on-Sea near Brighton, which he inherited from his mum, along with a nearby home. Because of something clever Prill's husband did with her will, Robbie thought I inherited my flat and fortune from a grateful customer from my shoe-shop days.

Confused? Try being me!

'Shall we test the coffee machine again?' said Fawn.

I laughed. 'It only arrived yesterday, and we've tested it so much it needs a service.'

'I want to perfect the cappuccino foam – it's not fluffy enough.'

'Okay, but just one, as my brain is racing from caffeine.'

Fawn was the coffee expert and worked magic with the massive, shiny red coffee machine which had the power of a Jumbo Jet – and sounded like one.

My efforts never equalled hers, probably as I was used to spooning Blandwell instant coffee into a mug and adding boiled water from the kettle.

As Fawn drove the machine, the divine aroma of fresh coffee beans delighted my nostrils as I surveyed our cafe, designed to resemble a yesteryear London with street-scene murals and cobbled-road effect flooring. We even had a row of colourful washing slung across the cafe, and the houses had real windowboxes abundant with colourful silk flowers.

Sat at a small, round cane table in a matching chair made comfy with a red gingham cushion, I heaved a satisfied, slightly smug sigh.

They say pride comes before a fall, and in my newfound state of bliss, I hoped it was a myth, and this was my new nirvanic lifestyle, a reward from the universe for years of boredom.

But I hoped there were no more murders to solve. One was enough.

Over cappuccinos and custard-cream biscuits, Fawn and I chatted about party plans.

'Let's keep it simple,' she suggested. 'Bucks Fizz, orange juice or water. With masses of vol au vents and sausages on sticks. Cheese and pineapple on sticks for the veggies.'

'Isn't that a little downmarket? If Princess Diana keeps her promise, we might have loads of posh people at the party.'

'We'll have loads anyway – this is Chelsea. Some might dress casually but be born with silver spoons in their mouths. Besides, the posher they are, the more they love everyday down-to-earth grub. All those highfalutin dinner parties full of grouse, pheasant, caviar and soufflé take their toll. Why do you think School Lunches is so popular?'

'School Lunches?'

'Yes – a restaurant where businessmen devour nursery-style food – all toad-in-the-hole and spotted dick. Tarquin loves School Lunches, although perhaps it's the waitresses dressed as schoolgirls which appeal more than the food. Anyway, trust me – simple food is fine if the alcohol flows. And we'll save money by diluting the champers with orange juice. Or we'll add peach juice instead and serve Bellinis. We'll switch to a cheaper fizz as the evening wears on, and if they want single-malt whisky, posh brandy or whatever, they can buy it from the bar.'

'I suppose so.' I thought back to various Christmases and New Years with their abundance of rich food and how I was desperate for plain food, like beans on toast, by January.

By the way, Tarquin was Fawn's wealthy boyfriend, financing Fawn's part of our new venture – for a cut of the profits. My funds were from the windfall I received from Prill.

Once the cafe opened, we planned a simple everyday menu of soup, sandwiches, cakes and pastries, most of which we would buy pre-made from a wonderful local catering company, Fast but Fabulous.

However, we'd serve a small shortbread biscuit (cookie if you're over the pond) with each tea or coffee. We would bake them with a drop of magical essence called Ojalis, which Prill used in her former cafe, Baking and Entering (now Robbie's antique shop). She'd said, 'Ojalis temporarily boosts mood and confidence. It wears off but doesn't have the toxic effect of drugs and alcohol. Regular use of Ojalis trains the mind to be more optimistic, so eventually, it's unnecessary. That's one reason my cafe was such a success.'

I hoped Scone but Not Forgotten would be a successful, happy venue.

But why did I feel something bad would happen soon?

Opening Night
Saturday, August 15th

After a day of heavy rain, opening night was balmy and pleasant. We threw open the double doors at 7 pm and greeted the small crowd gathered on the wide pavement. Although Fawn and I were welcoming and pleasant to everyone, I worried about the small turnout. Hidden in the kitchen, I hissed to Fawn, 'Hardly anyone is here.'

'Nah – don't worry – most will be fashionably late.'

'Most passers-by don't seem interested.'

'That's feigned nonchalance – they will be here in their droves over the next few days but are put off by the huge party banners, worried they weren't invited.'

'I guess.' In my panic, I hadn't thought of that. Deep down, I was still traumatised from the time nobody turned up for my tenth birthday party – until Mum realised she wrote my birthday's date on the invites, not the party planned for the week before.

Nevertheless, I was upset that even my neighbours and zany cleaner, Dolly, hadn't turned up for the opening party.

Fawn and I lived at 28 Queen Avenue, South Kensington – she in 28b, me in 28c. We'd invited Sebastian, a mid-twenties blonde cherub, from the ground floor and Peter, a mid-thirties opera singer from the top floor, where he cohabited with a large tank of tropical fish.

Sebastian, Peter and Dolly were involved in my first murder case, but that's another story. Literally.

As I topped up a distinguished middle-aged man's Bucks Fizz, a black cab pulled up outside, and Peter, Sebastian and Dolly hopped out, followed by Saphira, the talking cat. What was that naughty cat doing here? She'd promised to stay home.

'How did the cat get in the cab?' I asked my friends as Saphira glared as if to say, 'The cat? How dare you!'

'She must have sneaked in without us noticing,' said Dolly. 'The naughty girl.'

I couldn't ask Saphira in public as I (apart from Prill and her husband) was the only person who knew she could talk – and was magic and 200-years-old.

As she slinked in, imperious as usual, I glared at her as she put a paw to her lips, then hopped onto the counter as if onto a West End stage and proceeded to be the star of the show.

'I didn't know Cats was showing here tonight,' brayed a woman in a twinset and pearls. 'Isn't she adorable?'

From her beauty, it was apparent Saphira was female. I approached her and whispered, 'Meet me in the kitchen.'

Amazingly she followed me, sprang onto the closed freezer, and said, 'I'm here on a hunch to observe, as I believe there will be a murder in this vicinity soon.'

Muscles tensed, I said, 'Don't tease me, Saphira. One murder was enough. How do you know?'

'My extra-sensory cat perception.'

'Yes, I know, I know, honed over two hundred years. Is that all you have to go on?'

Outraged, she said, 'Is that all? That's akin to observing the Hanging Gardens of Babylon and saying, "Is that it?" What a cheek.'

With a giggle, I realised how commonplace a 200-year-old talking cat had become. In my recent former life of dullness, it would have amazed me. 'I'm sorry, your majesty. But so much incredible stuff has happened to me this year; it's become commonplace.'

She arched her back. 'Are you calling me common?'

'Far from it, your majesty. But you must see it my way.'

'Must I?'

'Oh, you know what I mean. Recently, I got divorced, inherited a posh flat and a fortune, and my friends include Prill, the ghost of my old friend who is also a witch, not to mention her dead husband – a warlock who still practices law – it's too much for little old me.'

Saphira narrowed her wise, gorgeous eyes. 'The universe would not choose you for such riches and responsibilities if you were not up to them.'

I guessed she was right. 'Thanks, your majesty.'

'Hey, it's Di, but for tonight and any future visits to your darling cafe, I'm Lady Elvira.'

I turned around to see a tall, dark-haired young woman with brown eyes, dressed in a gorgeous long black floaty number, I suspected by Ghost, brightened by a giant red feather boa at her long, slender neck.

'Were you just talking to that cat?' she said.

When I noticed Saphira bristle with indignation at 'that cat', I tried not to laugh.

But Saphira looked Lady Elvira in the eyes and said, 'Don't blow my cover, and I won't blow yours,' then she hopped onto the floor and went to join the merry, noisy crowd in the cafe.

I suspected Lady Elvira would be amazed, but she said, 'I always wanted to meet a talking cat. How divine.'

What a lovely woman – she had a charming, light-filled aura with a big dollop of mischief.

Lady Elvira held court, surrounded by many admirers, and appeared more royal than the Queen. By 9 pm, the evening was more disco than cafe opening.

But at 10 pm, a po-faced skinny man in a paisley-pattern silk dressing gown dashed in and barked, 'Keep the noise down. I'm trying to sleep.'

'And you are?' Dolly, clad in purple sequins, looked up as he towered over her five-foot-two height.

'Mr Creeper from the flat upstairs and the landlord of this establishment.'

'Would you like to dance?' said Dolly in a vain attempt to calm this curmudgeon.

'I don't dance – it's for morons.'

What a charmer.

'That's me told,' said Dolly as she wiggled her hips to 'Papa Don't Preach'.

My heart sank. Oh, no. Before then, Fawn and I had dealt with our landlord's mousy but pleasant wife, but her husband had the charm of Vlad the Impaler. Not that I'd met Vlad, but still. My wariness meter said Mr Creeper was trouble with a capital T.

'Would you like a glass of Bucks Fizz, sir?' I asked.

'I don't drink,' he snapped.

'Orange juice?'

'Bad for my digestion at this time of night. And turn that hideous music down or, preferably, off.'

'Papa Don't Preach' had morphed into 'Going Going Gone' on the cassette tape.

That was no way to talk about Bob Dylan – the man had no taste – Mr Creeper, not Mr Dylan. I've adored Bob since I was a teenager.

Mr Creeper's parting shot was, 'I'll be in at the usual time tomorrow and expect my usual lunch – a spa and a Waldorf.'

'But the menu has changed since it was Blossoms – we're more cafe than a restaurant...,' I began, but he'd walked away.

As I cursed, Fawn appeared and said, 'Drat. I thought I'd seen the last of that creep. His wife said he'd gone to work in Scotland – the Scots must have thrown him out.'

I knew what a Walford salad was from Fawlty Towers – celery, apple walnuts, grapes, but what the heck was a 'spa'?

'What's a spa when it's at home?' I asked Fawn.

'The silly sod means sparkling water, which he sips as he glares at customers drinking alcohol. He creates a terrible atmosphere, akin to a fire and brimstone preacher.'

'Should we organise a Waldorf salad for him?' I said, worried.

'No – let him choose from the new menu, and we might get rid of him.'

'Do we offer him a landlord discount?'

'Oh, yes – a hundred per cent – he never pays – never even leaves a tip, the stingy git. On second thoughts, we'd better add Waldorf salad to the menu as he's a right trouble maker.'

If I'd hated him before, I now hated him more, and his vile presence had left a sour taste in my mouth.

But the evening was too much fun to worry about misery guts, and Sebastian turned the volume back up. The possible ire of Mr Creeper was at the back of my mind, though, and I worried he'd reappear – a police officer in tow.

When I was chatting with Fawn at about 11 pm, a mousy little woman appeared in a brown sack-like dress that swamped her tiny frame – Mrs Creeper. She smiled meekly and addressed Fawn and me. 'Did my husband complain about the music earlier?'

'Yes,' said Fawn.

'I thought so – he said he'd only put out the rubbish. Anyway, he won't spoil your party as I slipped something into his cocoa.'

Strychnine, I hoped

'What did you slip in?' said Fawn.

'One of my sleeping pills.'

'Are you a light sleeper?' I said.

'Oh no, love. I sleep like a well-fed baby but lie to the doctor about bad insomnia. Those pills buy me a little time away from misery guts. And if he drives me mad during the day, I slip a tranquilliser into his tea.'

Not so mousy then.

Why did women (and some men) put up with such unpleasant spouses? I suppose money often comes into it when people get trapped by mortgages and joint possessions. And don't wish to upset the kids. Okay, my marriage hadn't been a romantic, passionate dream, but at least Steve was a nice person. And I was happy he'd found happiness with the new wife (a friend of mine) he'd recently married in Las Vegas.

And I adored my new boyfriend. That he lived in Sussex and I lived in London was a bonus as we'd both been trapped with the wrong partners and were enjoying a bit of freedom.

But whenever we got together, it was sexual dynamite because we were so in tune with one another. I'd waited long enough for it, and it was worth every former passion-free minute. Akin to endlessly waiting for Christmas as a child and Santa's gifts exceeding all your expectations.

Would my new venture exceed my expectations?

It Begins

Sunday, August 16th

Despite being tired, I awoke early and, with Saphira's help, made a massive batch of mini shortbread biscuits infused with magical vanilla essence we'd prepared three days earlier.

Saphira's help consisted of ordering me about and then incanting spells that sounded nonsensical such as,

When you bite into this shortbread most fab

You'll find the strength never to be drab

Your life will change

But only for the better

And you'll have the confidence

To enjoy life helter-skelter

Robbie drove to London, and we had a long, romantic Sunday lunch with all the trimmings in Julie's Restaurant in Holland Park. Then we went to my flat and spent a languorous afternoon and early evening in bed. At about 9 pm, he dressed, kissed my nose and said, 'Get an early night – big day tomorrow, and I wish you all the luck in the world.'

When he left, I had a jasmine-scented bubble bath, then lolled on the sofa and watched Crocodile Dundee. Again.

But no way could I wear Linda Kozlowski's revealing thong swimsuit without people snickering at my bum in all its wobbly glory.

Alone in bed, excited about opening day, I expected not to sleep. But as my head hit the pillow, the radio alarm woke me with 'Manic Monday'. Appropriate. Who wanted a quiet business launch apart from an earplug company?

Monday, August 17th

When Fawn and I arrived at Scone but Not Forgotten, I was surprised and pleased to see nearly everything organised by Lynn, the manager, and two cheerful Australian waitresses.

I'd been reluctant to leave them to it, but Fawn, with her usual wisdom beyond her years (a tad annoying, sometimes), had said, 'If you don't show people you trust them, they don't work as hard, and if you hover over people, it drains their confidence.'

Nothing could drain Lynn's confidence and I found her a tad overbearing. If I weren't careful, she would boss me, and I'd had enough of being a doormat. Deciding to start as I meant to go on, let her know who was boss, I said, 'Shall we sit at this window table and survey our kingdom before we start, Fawn?'

She nodded. 'Good idea. I'll order cappuccinos from Evie.'

Evie was a friendly Italian girl and a maestro on the coffee machine. 'People who love coffee make great coffee, and Evie lives on the stuff,' Fawn said before we employed her.

After a divine sip of perfect cappuccino topped with flaked chocolate, I said, 'This is even better than yours, Fawn.'

'Cheek – but you're right. In busy times Evie can be at the coffee and tea station permanently. It's more efficient that way.'

'Are you sure?' Evie was too gorgeous to be hidden behind a wall of steam.

'Yes – trust me.'

Before we started Scone but Not Forgotten, Fawn was the manager of Blossoms Cafe on the same premises. Having no cafe experience, apart from eating in them, I'd bowed down to most of Fawn's ideas. So we had an entire staff who could run things if neither of us was there. And while we both had designated tasks, it left us free to step in when necessary.

We planned to work four days a week apiece with alternate weekends off, leaving Fawn free to date Tarquin and me to date Robbie in London or Sussex.

At Fawn's suggestion, our jobs were to greet customers, sit with them if they asked, have beady eyes out for problems and be ready to step into the breach.

I was a little dubious and worried I'd feel lazy, but Fawn said, 'You'll laugh at that notion by the end of today.'

I did.

Later, when I realised the amount of red tape and paperwork involved, I ate my naïve words.

When we opened the doors, people flooded in and claimed all the tables within minutes. Poor Evie was hidden behind a wall of steam as she frothed milk, made coffee and brewed tea, and I wished I'd worn running shoes as I sped from table-to-table dispensing egg and bacon sandwiches, croissants, coffees and teas.

Between that, I cleared tables and rushed empty glasses, cups, saucers and plates into the kitchen to be washed by the kitchen porter.

Despite the fast-paced craziness, the atmosphere was electric, and I'd never been happier at work.

As we passed each other running in opposite directions, Fawn said, 'Blossoms was never this busy. Reckon I've underestimated staff and food requirements.'

'A good problem to have,' I shouted over my shoulder.

It was so busy that I had to nip to Marks and Spencer in the afternoon to stock up on food and felt idiotic pushing an overloaded trolley along King's Road.

'You must be hungry, love,' shouted a young man with spiky black hair streaked with fluorescent pink.

'Is that your husband's lunch?' quipped a stylish fifty-ish woman.

'Yes – he's a greedy boy,' I said.

Life was great fun, with never a dull moment.

What could go wrong?

Carry on reading Scone but Not Forgotten[1]

---

1. https://books2read.com/sconebutnotforgotten

About the Author

Thank you for reading this book.

I hope you enjoyed it as much as I loved writing it. If so, if you could spare a few moments to leave a quick review on the relevant bookseller site, I would be most grateful.

Please visit my website to discover more of my fun books (link below). While you're there, I'd love you to sign up for my newsletter, Janet's VIP Readers, so you don't miss out on new releases, freebies and offers.

Thanks again.

Janet xx

Read more at www.janetbutlermale.co.uk.

Printed in Great Britain
by Amazon